New places, new people...

"So Salvador, do you want to hang out?" Erin asked. "We can check out the hotel—maybe even sneak out and see some sights."

I hesitated for a second, thinking about all the studying I hadn't done for the competition tomorrow. Then I glanced at Erin and almost smacked myself on the head. *What kind of lunatic would turn this girl down?* I wondered.

Not this one.

"I'm in," I told her, trying to sound as casual as she did. "Maybe we can even sneak out of the dinner early."

Suddenly this trip was looking up. *Way* up.

Don't miss any of the books in SWEET VALLEY JUNIOR HIGH, an exciting series from Bantam Books!

Three Days, Two Nights

Written by
Jamie Suzanne

Created by
FRANCINE PASCAL

BANTAM BOOKS
NEW YORK · TORONTO · LONDON · SYDNEY · AUCKLAND

RL 4, 008-012

THREE DAYS, TWO NIGHTS
A Bantam Book / January 2000

Sweet Valley Junior High is a trademark of Francine Pascal.
Conceived by Francine Pascal.
Cover photography by Michael Segal.

Produced by 17th Street Productions, Inc.
33 West 17th Street
New York, NY 10011.

ISBN: 0-553-48701-9

Visit us on the Web! www.randomhouse.com/kids

Published simultaneously in the United States and Canada

Bantam Books is an imprint of Random House Children's Books, a
division of Random House, Inc. BANTAM BOOKS and the rooster
colophon are registered trademarks of Random House, Inc. Bantam Books,
1540 Broadway, New York, New York 10036.

PRINTED IN THE UNITED STATES OF AMERICA

OPM   0 9 8 7 6 5 4 3 2 1

To Margaret Abigail Chardiet

Salvador

"Hey, Salvador!" Brian Rainey gave me a friendly punch on the arm as he passed my locker after school. "You heading out?"

"Just a sec," I said as I slammed the locker door shut. I slung my backpack over my shoulder. "Actually, I need to check out the student-events bulletin board real quick."

"Oh yeah? Which of the upcoming school events are you interested in, exactly?" Brian asked, his green eyes twinkling with amusement.

"The results of those tests we had to take last week are supposed to be posted this afternoon," I said, turning to walk down the hallway. All the eighth-graders at Sweet Valley Junior High had taken academic-aptitude tests in six different subjects. The principal said it was for some kind of statewide competition or something.

Brian followed me down the crowded hallway, dodging a group of jocks on their way to practice.

"Yeah, I remember those tests, all right," he told me, shaking his head. "Just check the bottom of the lists for my name." He shrugged good-naturedly. "Standardized tests aren't exactly my forte."

Usually when I take a test in class, I end up guessing on at least half of the questions. Or I just can't resist putting down funny answers instead of real ones. One of the questions on my last history test was about agriculture and livestock in ancient Rome. So I wrote my whole answer in pig latin. Needless to say, my teacher was *not* amused.

And that was pretty much how most of those academic tests went for me last week. I did some major guessing on the math and history sections. And the literature and foreign-language parts weren't a whole lot better. I did a little better in geography—you don't have two parents who travel all over the place for their military jobs without picking up the basics—but I choked on the state capitals. I mean, who can remember the difference between Montgomery and Montpelier anyway? I've got more important things to think about. But the science part was different. I *knew* the answers. Like, pretty much *all* of them.

"Whoa!" Brian stopped short as we rounded a corner and came within sight of the bulletin board. At least three dozen kids were already gathered around the test results.

"Come on." Brian was already moving forward

through the crowd, trying to get close enough to see the list tacked to the bulletin board. "Let's check out the damage."

I started to follow him and ended up stepping on some girl's foot. "Excuse me," I said as she glared at me. I shot her an apologetic grin, then craned my neck. Brian was way ahead of me, near the front of the crowd. "Hey, Bri. Can you see?"

"Uh-huh," Brian called over his shoulder.

I wriggled my way between a couple of tall girls and reached Brian's side just in time to hear him whistle softly.

"Check it out!" he exclaimed, jabbing a finger at one of the sheets of paper.

"What?" I asked, trying to see what he was pointing at. "Did you do better than you thought?"

"No, not me, *you*." Brian smiled at me. I focused in on the names on the list, searching for mine. Slowly I raised my eyes up, up, up. . . .

My mouth dropped open.

"No way," I said, staring at Brian in shock.

I gasped, reading the words again.

Salvador del Valle, 97 percent. Top scorer—science.

"Wait, did you see this?" Brian's voice finally broke into my stupor. He was inspecting a notice hanging above all the test scores.

I squinted at the sheet of paper, quickly scanning it. "It says . . . the top scorers all go to

Sacramento for a—wait, an *academic tournament?*"

"Yeah, isn't that cool?" Brian asked. "You get a free weekend in Sacramento."

A weekend in Sacramento? An academic tournament? So *that* was what those tests had been for? Why did Brian think that was so great? I mean, who wanted to spend a whole weekend trapped with a bunch of overachievers when I could be right here in Sweet Valley, underachieving as usual?

"Hey, Sal," Brian said, scanning the other lists. "Guess who else is—"

"Hi," Elizabeth Wakefield's breathless voice interrupted him. I spun around and saw her standing next to Anna Wang. As usual, Elizabeth looked fantastic. And as usual, seeing her gave me this little jolt of excitement. Her long, blond hair was pulled back in these cute little hair things shaped like butterflies, and her blue-green eyes were sparkling with interest. I've known Anna practically my whole life, but I just met Elizabeth this year, when she was rezoned from her old middle school to SVJH. The three of us have all become really good friends, though. We do almost everything together.

"So have you seen our names anywhere?" Elizabeth asked.

I flashed a grin, excited to share the news of my one and only shining academic moment.

"Get this," I began, catching Anna's eye.

"Good news, Wakefield," Brian cut in. "You blew everyone away on the English-lit section."

Elizabeth looked at the list and clapped her hands over her mouth. "Oh my God, I got the top score!" she exclaimed.

"Congratulations." Anna beamed at her. "That's amazing."

"You think *that's* amazing?" I said, clearing my throat. "Take a look at this." I pointed at the sheet with the science scores, glancing again at my name on the top. Oh yeah.

Anna followed my gaze, then blinked in surprise. "Wow," she said. "Is that for real?"

"Yeah, who knew good old Salvador was such a genius, huh?" Brian kidded.

"Thanks for all the support, guys," I said, glaring at Brian.

Anna and Brian laughed, but Elizabeth just looked excited. "Salvador, that is so great," she said. "I never knew you were so good at science."

I almost blushed. It takes a lot to impress a girl like Elizabeth Wakefield. I should know—I certainly tried back at the beginning of school, when I had a giant crush on her. But she seemed really thrilled for me. And, well, really *impressed*.

"Who else got top scores?" Anna asked. "Did you see?"

Brian frowned. "Sorry, Anna," he said.

I could see a hint of disappointment in Anna's dark brown eyes, but she quickly covered it up.

"I've been to Sacramento before," she said. "It was pretty boring. I just thought it would be cool to go with you guys," she said.

Anna's really smart, but with all the people taking the tests, it must have been hard to get the top scores.

Yeah, and I actually did it, I thought in amazement.

"Well, at least *you* won't be bored in Sacramento," Brian said to me with a shrug as we all wandered away from the crowd. "You and Elizabeth can hang out together."

"Yeah, this trip is going to be so much fun, don't you think?" Elizabeth asked me.

Suddenly it started to sink in. Elizabeth and I would be away together for an entire weekend. It wouldn't be like usual, with me and her and Anna doing stuff together—working on *Zone*, this 'zine the three of us started a while ago with Brian, or watching videos, or going to the mall. It would be just me and Elizabeth, all alone in an exciting new place. No parents. No school. Just us.

I shot a glance at Elizabeth, wondering if she was thinking anything along those lines. I think maybe she was because when we locked eyes, she began to blush.

"Uh, I'd better go," she said a little nervously. She checked her watch. "I don't want to miss my bus."

"Right," I said a little too quickly. "Hey, and don't forget to tell the Jessinator I said hi."

Usually Elizabeth rolls her eyes or looks exasperated when I make fun of her twin sister, Jessica. But today she completely ignored it. "Uh-huh," she said. "Okay, well, bye."

Elizabeth hurried off to her bus, and I followed Brian and Anna outside, barely listening to their conversation.

I couldn't stop thinking about this Sacramento trip, and how it would just be me and Elizabeth. I've always liked her. A lot. And I'm pretty sure she's always felt the same way about me. We even kissed a couple of times. But then Anna freaked out when she found out about us kissing, so Elizabeth and I agreed to be just friends. Anna and I have been best friends forever, so I guess she felt pretty left out.

I glanced over at Anna and Brian just as Anna burst out laughing at something Brian said.

Anna's totally over that now, I thought. The three of us had been getting along fine, and we were all *just friends*.

But once you start liking someone, you can't just *stop*. A weekend alone with Elizabeth, without Anna around, could change everything.

7

Jessica

"So then Mr. Wilfred asked what I was staring at," I told Kristin Seltzer as we walked toward my locker.

Kristin giggled, twirling one finger in her blond hair. "Yeah?" she prompted. "So did you tell him the truth?"

"Right!" I snorted and spun the combination on my locker. I dumped my books on the top shelf, then turned to face Kristin. "What was I going to say—'Sorry, Mr. Wilfred, but I was looking out the window to keep from going into a coma because your class is so boring'? So Damon Ross happened to be out in the hallway, and I was checking out how amazingly gorgeous my sort-of boyfriend looked." I rolled my eyes. "I'm just lucky I wasn't actually *drooling!*"

Kristin laughed again. "Definitely lucky."

I smiled, closing my eyes for a second as I remembered seeing Damon in the hallway, his incredible blue eyes, thick brown hair, broad shoulders. . . .

"Jessica! Great news!"

I opened my eyes. A decidedly nondreamy sight faced me. Namely my locker partner, Ronald Rheece.

Ronald is what my parents call "a fine young man" and my twin sister, Elizabeth, calls "a really nice, sweet guy." In other words, a hopeless nerd.

"Ronald," I said with a sigh. "Kristin and I are in the middle of something."

Ronald didn't seem to hear me. His big, puppy-dog eyes were glittering with excitement, and his skinny little arms were shaking. I mean, literally *shaking*. I took half a step back just in case he had something contagious.

"It's just such a dream come true!" he exclaimed. "I can't believe this is happening!"

"What is it, Ronald?" Kristin asked politely. Sometimes she can be way too nice.

Ronald clasped his hands together and smiled gleefully. "I got the top score on the math part of the aptitude test," he explained, as if he'd just been the first nerd to walk on Neptune or something. "That means I get to go to the state academic competition in Sacramento."

"Hey, that's great!" Kristin said sincerely, reaching over to pat him on the shoulder. "Congratulations, Ronald."

"Yeah, that's nice," I said, already turning back

to Kristin to continue our conversation.

Unfortunately Ronald wasn't finished pestering us yet. "Yes, I almost qualified in science as well," he said thoughtfully. "But I guess I focused too much on the physics and chemistry parts of the test. I'm a little weak in biology."

You can say that again, I thought, glancing at his scrawny body and pencil neck.

"I'm sure that's why I got only ninety-six percent on the science section," he mused. "And Salvador del Valle got ninety-seven percent."

That got my attention.

"Wait a minute," I said. "You mean El Salvador was the top scorer in something other than annoying me and cracking lame jokes? Unbelievable." Even though he was friends with my genius sister, I'd never exactly thought of Salvador as the academic type. More like the irritating, immature type.

"I'm sorry, Jessica," Ronald said with a sincerely apologetic expression. "I checked the list quite thoroughly, and you didn't make it." He watched me carefully like he thought I would burst into tears. Like I would actually be sad at not being chosen to go to some nerd fest. "Um, your sister had a top score, though."

"Really?" I asked, not too surprised. "Let me guess. English, right?" Elizabeth has always been really into reading books and writing papers.

Ronald nodded. "Literature, actually."

"Who else got chosen?" Kristin asked, picking a piece of fluff off the sleeve of her flowered T-shirt.

Ronald ticked off the names on his fingers. "Richard Griggs for history. Bernadette So, geography. And Bethel McCoy, oral foreign language."

"Bethel made it? Wow, she must be so excited," I said. Bethel is on the track team with me—that's how we became friends. She's the best runner on the team, and she's really competitive—in everything. I knew this would mean a lot to her.

"Jess? Isn't your bus leaving, like, now?" Kristin asked.

I glanced up at the clock on the wall.

"Oh no," I said. I hoisted my backpack up onto my shoulder. "Gotta run," I said as I bolted to the exit.

"See ya, Jess," Kristin called after me.

"Until tomorrow, Jessica," Ronald added.

Ronald is just *so* weird.

I made it to the bus barely in time, and I sank down into the empty seat next to Elizabeth right before the bus driver started to pull out of the SVJH parking lot.

"So, congratulations," I said, giving Elizabeth a playful shove. "I hear my sister the brain won a ticket to a weekend of fun-filled tests!"

"Thanks." Elizabeth smiled. "I know this isn't

11

your idea of excitement," she said, "but I think it could be a lot of fun."

"You do?" I shrugged, amazed as always at the things my twin found interesting. "Well, yeah, if you *like* being surrounded by a bunch of geeks from all over the state. No offense."

"Uh-huh, yeah," she said, staring off into space.

I waved my hand in front of her face.

"Hello? Liz? Aren't you going to jump on my case and give me a long, boring lecture about using the "*g*" word to talk about people who are—what is it—socially challenged?"

Elizabeth just kept smiling dreamily, kind of like the way I get when I'm thinking about Damon.

Suddenly something hit me.

"Hold it," I said. "You're going to be in Sacramento with Salvador. Is that why you're acting all goofy?"

Elizabeth's face turned bright red. "Actually," she said haughtily, "I think that this is a great opportunity to represent our school. And I want to—"

"Uh-huh," I interrupted. Folding my arms over my chest, I sat back against the fake-leather bus seat. "Truth?"

"Okay, okay," she blurted out. "So maybe I'm a *little* excited about the idea of spending a whole weekend away with Salvador."

I grinned. Frankly, I think Salvador is extremely

annoying, but I like to see my sister lose her cool once in a while—and Salvador definitely manages to accomplish that.

"Don't get me wrong," Elizabeth added hastily. "Salvador and I are just friends now." She leaned back against the bus window, and the silly smile crept back over her face.

"Yeah, but you never know what could happen," I said, nudging her with my elbow.

"You never know," Elizabeth agreed dreamily.

I had a feeling Sacramento was going to be a lot more interesting than I'd thought.

Dear Parent,

We are pleased to inform you that your son or daughter has been selected to represent Sweet Valley Junior High at the Statewide Academic Challenge in Sacramento. Please sign the attached permission slip, which also includes the pickup and drop-off times and other important scheduling information.

In addition to the competition, which will take place on Saturday and Sunday from 9 A.M. to 3 P.M., the weekend will include other activities such as a visit to our state capitol building. Students will also have an opportunity to meet the best and brightest from junior-high schools all over the state.

All activities will be strictly chaperoned, so your child will be in good hands throughout the weekend. We trust this trip will be a unique and educational experience for everyone involved.

Sincerely,
Albert Todd
Principal,
Sweet Valley Junior High School

Damon

I raced up the front walk and burst through the front door of our trailer, hoping to have more than the usual two seconds with my mom before she left for work. She works nights as a waitress at a nearby diner, and normally she zips away as soon as I get home.

"Damon!" My mom hardly had time to gasp out my name before I barreled into her, almost knocking her halfway across our tiny living room.

"Oops!" I grabbed her arm just in time to stop her from tumbling over the coffee table. "Sorry. Are you okay?"

She shook her arm free of my grip and brushed herself off, then shot me a glance that was half annoyed, half amused.

"Where's the fire?"

I grinned sheepishly. "Um, I wanted to ask you something before you went to work."

"Uh-oh," she joked. "Sounds big."

I shrugged, then followed her as she headed back into the kitchen, which was really just another section of the trailer's long, narrow main room.

"Actually, I was wondering if I could invite someone over on Friday night. You know, to help me baby-sit Kaia and Sally while you're at work."

"Someone?" She raised an eyebrow and started unloading the dishes from the drying rack next to the sink. "Would this be a female someone? Perhaps the same blond female someone who baby-sat the girls recently?"

"Maybe," I muttered, blushing. I grabbed a couple of plates and put them away in the cabinet.

I'd been thinking about it all day—how to find a way to spend more time with Jessica. My mom can't afford to pay a baby-sitter to watch my sisters, so I'm pretty much stuck at home most of the time, except for Saturdays and Sundays. Sometimes even those days I can't go out, like if another waitress calls in sick and my mom has to cover for her. Jessica got along really well with my sisters this one time she watched them by herself, so I figured inviting her over would be a great way to get *them* to stop asking me when she was coming again and to spend more time with Jessica.

"Of course you can have Jessica over," my mom told me, flashing me an understanding smile. "The girls will be thrilled." She paused as she stacked the last plate onto the pile. She closed the cabinet door, then turned around to face me.

"But I won't be at work on Friday night, by the way."

"Huh?" I felt a moment of panic. Had Mom lost her job? That would be seriously bad news. Ever since my dad split years ago, money had been a major problem.

She was still smiling, so I relaxed a little.

"I switched with one of the other waitresses to get the night off," she explained. "I—I have a date."

"A what?" I asked, confused. "You mean, you have plans?"

She laughed, then reached up to ruffle my hair.

"I have a *date*. With a man."

I blinked, then swallowed hard as the words sank in. My mom hadn't gone out with a *man* since . . . well, never. Unless you count my dad. But that's different—they were *married*.

Her smile faded a little as she watched me, waiting for my reaction.

"Really?" I finally asked, wondering what she wanted me to say. "Uh, so who's the guy?"

"It's Ben," she replied, brightening up again. "Remember? He's Betty's brother." Betty's one of the waitresses my mom works with. "You've met him a couple times at the diner," she continued. I had? I couldn't think of what he looked like. "He stops by there a lot. Well, at least he has a lot *lately*."

Was it my imagination, or was she . . . blushing? I narrowed my eyes for a closer inspection.

Damon

Sure enough, her cheeks were slightly pink.

"Um, so how did this, uh, date happen?" I asked.

She shrugged. "Well, he's been staying late to talk to me after my shift. And then yesterday he suggested that we get together outside of the diner." She blushed again, looking happy and sort of shy, like someone *my* age with a crush.

Then she glanced at me and grinned. "Anything else you'd like to know—*Dad?*"

I let out a deep breath. My mom could tease me all she wanted, but I wasn't about to let her go out with some stranger without at least getting some basic information.

"Yeah," I said. "So where are you going? On your date, I mean."

She frowned. "Probably to a movie," she answered. "And dinner. I know it's been a while, but people still do that stuff, right?"

I cringed—my mom was asking *me* about what people do on dates? How messed up. I mean, I knew I should be happy for her. When she said the guy's name, her whole face glowed. And if anyone I know deserves to glow like that, it's my mom.

But I couldn't help worrying about what would happen if something went wrong. When my dad left, my mom was a complete mess for a long time.

I wasn't about to let anyone else hurt her like that.

But what could I do to stop it?

Phone Conversation the Night Before the Trip to Sacramento

Bethel: Hello?

Jameel: Hey, Bethel, it's me.

Bethel: Hey. Listen, I've got to go memorize some verbs. I'll call you as soon as I'm back Sunday night, okay?

Jameel: Okay . . . I'm going to miss you so much.

Bethel: It's just a weekend.

Jameel: Maybe you could call from Sacramento.

Bethel: It's just one weekend! Look, I have to go.

Jameel: Good luck. I'll write you while you're gone, okay?

Bethel: Good night, Jameel.

Jameel: Bye.

[Pause]

Bethel: Why didn't you hang up?

Jameel: Why didn't you?

Bethel: I'm hanging up now. . . .

[Pause]

Jameel: Still there?

Bethel: Jameel, I have to go!

Jameel: So hang up. We'll do it together. One, two, three . . .

[Pause]

Bethel: Jameel?

Jameel: Yeah?

Bethel: I'll miss you too.

Salvador

The minute my grandmother, the Doña, walked into the kitchen on Friday morning and saw me stuffing toast into my mouth, her eyebrows shot up in surprise.

"Salvador," she said. "You're up early."

I grinned at her through a mouthful of crumbs. "Uh-huh." I swallowed. "Don't want to miss the bus to Sacramento. The field trip, remember?"

I'm not really a morning person. Normally the Doña has to practically toss me out the window to get me to wake up. I wondered if she had any inkling of the real reason I was so psyched for this trip.

"Don't forget to chew, Salvador," she told me, shaking her head.

I just nodded and grabbed another slice of toast. "See you Sunday night," I said, grabbing my backpack.

She wrapped me up in a big hug and blurted out a few last-minute warnings and instructions.

"Good luck," she said as I finally headed out the door. It took me a second to realize she

20

meant with the academic competition.

It was probably the first time in my life that I was ever early for school—or anything else, for that matter, except maybe lunch. I was so early that the charter bus that was supposed to pick us up wasn't even there yet. Neither were any of the other kids.

Eventually the regular school buses started pulling in. I spotted Elizabeth's bus before it made the turn—I'd memorized the number by the second week of school.

I waited patiently while about a million other kids ambled off the bus as slowly as possible. Finally Elizabeth appeared. She spotted me right away and waved. Jessica was right behind her. She sort of smirked at me as she walked past with her gym bag slung over one shoulder. "Have fun this weekend, El Salvador," she sang out.

I didn't bother to respond. Jessica was already halfway across the lawn anyway. "So, hey," I said when Elizabeth reached me. "Are you, uh, ready?"

She smiled and set her suitcase on the sidewalk beside my duffel bag. "I hope so," she answered. "I've been studying all week, but there's so much to know."

Studying?

"Yeah," I said, trying not to seem surprised. "I've been studying a lot too."

That was a total load. I hadn't cracked a book

21

all week. But I didn't want to sound like a slacker.

Elizabeth checked her watch. "The bus should be here soon."

"Uh-huh." I swallowed hard. "Um, so should we sit together? On the bus, I mean."

Elizabeth smiled again. "Of course," she said.

"Cool." I nodded, kicking at the ground with my shoe.

"Hey, there's Berna," Elizabeth said, glancing behind me. I turned and saw Bernadette So approaching us, carrying an overnight bag.

"Hi," she said in her soft, shy voice. Bernadette's been at SVJH for as long as I have, but I don't know her that well. She's really shy—like, almost pathologically shy. I couldn't help wondering how she was going to survive this contest. One time last year she had to give a speech in English class, and her face got so red, I was sure she was going to spontaneously combust.

"Yo, Berna," I greeted her. "Hey, do you know Elizabeth Wakefield?"

Bernadette smiled timidly at Elizabeth. "Um, not really," she said, tucking a couple of strands of her curly, chin-length dark hair behind one ear. "I've seen you around, though."

"Me too." Elizabeth gave her a warm smile. She's nice to everyone—that's just one of the great things about her. "Glad to meet you.

What subject are you competing in again?"

"Geography," Bernadette practically whispered. "You're English lit, right?"

Elizabeth nodded, but before she could say anything, Ronald Rheece came rushing up to us, carrying a cotton duffel bag with pictures of rocket ships printed all over it. No joke.

"Greetings, all!" he exclaimed breathlessly, tossing his bag on top of mine. "I can't believe this day is finally here! I was reading up on the state capitol building last night on the Internet, and it sounds really fascinating. Did you know that it was built in 1869, and there are hallway displays for each of California's counties inside? Also, it's in this big park with lots of gardens, including a rose garden and a bunch of camellias—which are the official city flower of Sacramento, by the way. . . ."

I glanced at Elizabeth, who was nodding and listening politely as Ronald babbled on and on.

Okay, so far this kind of stinks, I thought. All this time I'd been excited at the idea of being alone with Elizabeth for the weekend.

But I'd forgotten something—we *weren't* going to be alone.

Elizabeth

I tried to pay attention to what Ronald was saying about the state capitol building, but it wasn't easy. The whole time I kept wondering if this weekend was going to be anything at all like I'd imagined.

I'd kind of looked forward to some quality time with Salvador, away from our everyday lives. *I guess I forgot about the other people on our team,* I thought, doing my best to nod and smile at the right times so Ronald wouldn't realize I wasn't paying attention.

At least Salvador and I would be sitting together on the bus. And it was a long drive up to Sacramento—we would have plenty of time to talk.

"Hi, guys!" Bethel McCoy called, interrupting Ronald's explanation of the construction of the capitol rotunda.

Turning, I saw Bethel jog up the sidewalk. Even in her baggy jeans and sweatshirt she still looked really graceful and athletic when she ran.

"Hi, Bethel," I greeted her. Jessica's good

friends with Bethel, but I don't talk to her that much. She just seems so, I don't know, *intense*.

"Am I the last one here?" Bethel asked, shrugging off her oversized leather backpack and then running one hand over her hair.

Ronald shook his head. "No," he said. "Richard isn't here yet."

"Yes, he is," a voice resounded from across the street.

Glancing up, I saw Richard Griggs loping toward us. All I knew about Richard was that he was Bethel's locker partner. Jessica had informed me that he'd be the one "cool" guy on the trip. Watching him approach, I couldn't help noticing that he *was* really good-looking. He has wavy, brown hair and intense green eyes. When he said hello and flashed a lopsided, cocky grin, I saw that his teeth were perfectly straight except for one on the bottom that was just a tiny bit crooked. It made his face seem even better looking somehow.

"Glad you could finally make it, Griggs," Bethel said.

Richard chuckled. "Yeah, right, McCoy," he responded. "I saw you booking down the street right in front of me."

"It's a good thing we're all here on time," Ronald said. "We have a long ride in front of us. I checked on the Internet, and according to my calculations it will take us slightly over six hours to travel to Sacramento."

"Does that allow for traffic developments?" Salvador asked, his face in a mock-serious expression. I stifled a giggle. Salvador can always make me laugh.

"So where are the chaperons?" Bethel asked, glancing at her watch. "We're supposed to leave soon."

"Maybe they decided not to come," Salvador suggested. He pumped his fist in the air. "Par-tay!"

Ronald shook his head. "No," he said sternly. "Ms. Upton and Mr. Martinez are definitely coming. It was on the permission slip."

"Anyway, this weekend isn't about partying," Bethel told Salvador with a little frown. "We're going up there to try to win this competition for our school. Remember?"

"Ooookay," Salvador said, holding up both hands. "Whatever."

He rolled his eyes at me behind Bethel's back. I shrugged in return. It wasn't like I totally disagreed with Bethel—I mean, the academic competition *was* the whole reason behind this trip, and we all wanted to win. Of course, that didn't mean we weren't allowed to have any fun at the same time. . . .

Just then I heard the sound of grinding gears and turned to see a big, silver bus taking the turn into the school parking lot. It drove over to the curb and stopped in front of us. Through the large, tinted windows I could see kids our age looking out at us.

"Check out our ride," Salvador said, letting out a low whistle. "So this is how the smart half lives?"

I sighed and gave him a light punch on the shoulder. I hate how he's always so down on himself. You'd think after getting the top score on the science test, he'd finally take himself more seriously.

That's silly, I reminded myself. Salvador doesn't take *anything* seriously. It's why I like him so much—he keeps me from being *too* serious.

"Who are all those other people?" Salvador asked, staring up at the bus.

"Didn't you read the schedule they gave us?" I asked.

Salvador grinned. "Um, not exactly," he said. "I made it into a paper airplane on my way home. It flew pretty far too."

I couldn't help laughing. Typical Salvador.

"This bus is picking up kids from all the schools in this county," I explained.

Just then our chaperons, Ms. Upton and Mr. Martinez, came hurrying out of the school building. Ms. Upton clapped and called for our attention. "All right, everyone," she announced. She examined the clipboard in her hand. "Please line up and board the bus in an orderly fashion. Mr. Martinez and I will point you toward your seats—some of the other schools are already on board, but we still have several other stops to make. There will be room in the overhead bins to store your bags."

Salvador raised his hand in salute. "Yes, sir!" he shouted. "Uh, I mean, ma'am."

Ms. Upton shot him an exasperated look, but she didn't respond. She was too busy herding us into a straight line. I took my place between Salvador and Bethel.

When we climbed on the bus, I saw that there were about twenty kids from other schools already on board. Most of them didn't pay much attention to us as we headed down the aisle. A lot of them were sleeping or drinking sodas or talking to one another. A few were studying. I couldn't help wondering which of them would be competing against me in English lit.

Mr. Martinez pointed out our seats, which were near the back of the bus. Then he returned to the front and sat down with Ms. Upton and some chaperons from the other schools.

"Cool," Salvador whispered, leaning over my shoulder and speaking into my ear as we waited for Ronald to sling his bag into the overhead compartment. His breath tickled a little bit. "If the chaperons sit up front, they won't be able to see what we're doing."

Bethel heard him and rolled her eyes. "What do you have planned, del Valle?" she asked. "Plotting to overthrow the government or something?"

Salvador looked wounded. "You say that like I couldn't actually do it."

I laughed. "Come on," I told him. "Let's sit here." I started to hoist my suitcase toward the rack overhead.

"Please, allow me." Salvador grabbed it out of my hands. "I'll take care of it. You want the window?"

"Sure. Thanks." I slid into the seat, which was about a thousand times more comfortable than the ones on the normal school bus I take every day. It even had a footrest and a little table that folded down, like on an airplane.

Bethel and Ronald took the seat behind us, and Richard and Bernadette sat right across the aisle from them.

"Here we go," Ronald exclaimed, bouncing up and down in his seat. "I can't wait till we get there!"

Bethel flashed him an annoyed glance. "Ronald," she said sharply, "if you're going to sit with me, you've got to sit still. I need to study on the ride up, and I can't concentrate with you jumping around like a crazy kangaroo."

One thing you can say for Bethel—she tells it like it is. Ronald settled down, but his eyes sort of lost their spark, and his face sagged.

"Sorry," he told Bethel. "I'll try to sit still."

I felt kind of sorry for him. He was obviously really excited about the trip, and Bethel was making that seem like some kind of crime. *Bethel is even more intense than I realized,* I thought, glancing at her. She was already shuffling through her bag and pulling out books. *I guess she takes academics just as seriously as she takes track.* Jessica's always saying how Bethel pushes herself really hard in races and gets all frustrated when she thinks she could have done better.

As Salvador finished shoving both of our bags into the overhead compartment, I couldn't help noticing that he looked especially cute in his khakis and rugby shirt. When he sat down next to me, he sort of bumped into me with one elbow, and I got a weird, tingly feeling on my arm where we touched.

"Well," he said as the bus roared to life and pulled slowly away from the curb. "Here we go."

I don't know why, but I started to feel nervous. Nervous and excited. Pretty soon I'd be bouncing around like a kangaroo and Bethel would have to yell at me.

How to Get Sick of Your Friend in One Short Hour

7:15 A.M.   As the bus pulls out of the school parking lot, Elizabeth and Salvador start chatting enthusiastically about *Zone*. "That article you wrote about sharing lockers is awesome," Salvador tells her. "It's going to be the best thing in the whole 'zine!" "It's not that great," Elizabeth insists. "But that cartoon you drew about the secrets of the teachers' lounge—that's hilarious."

7:36 A.M.   After talking about *Zone,* the Doña's fencing-class mishaps, the latest changes in the cafeteria menu, and then *Zone* again, Elizabeth and Salvador sit in awkward silence. "Tickle fight!" Salvador yells, leaning over and tickling Elizabeth under her arms. Elizabeth shrieks with laughter and does her best to tickle him back. The tickle fight ends when Bethel leans forward and smacks Salvador on the back of the head, demanding that they keep it down so she can study.

7:48 A.M.   Salvador wonders why Elizabeth isn't

saying anything. Then he wonders why he can't think of anything to say to her. Then he wonders what anyone, anywhere, anytime in the history of the world could possibly have to say to anyone else. "Uh, it looks like it's going to be nice and sunny today," he says lamely in a desperate attempt to break the silence. "Yes," Elizabeth replies. Then she turns to look out the window, and Salvador starts biting his thumbnail.

8:02 A.M. "So," Elizabeth finally says. "Sacramento is the capital of California. Did you know that the golden poppy is our state flower?" "Uh, no," Salvador replies.

8:16 A.M. Ronald leans over and brightly suggests that they all play a game. "How about the ABC game?" he suggests. "Or maybe the license-plate game. My family always plays that on long car trips." Salvador and Elizabeth eagerly agree to play the game—any game, as long as they will *all* be playing.

Bethel

"So, what should we play?" Ronald asked me.

I sighed. "Count me out," I told him. "*One* of us should actually be studying." I stared at the others pointedly.

"I can't read on the bus," Salvador whined. "It makes me puke."

"What are we playing?" Ronald repeated, bouncing anxiously in his seat.

"How about truth or dare?" Richard suggested. "But it would be better if we had an equal number of guys and girls. . . ."

I tried to tune them out and focus on the Spanish verb conjugations on the page in front of me. But for some reason I just couldn't concentrate—I hadn't been able to this whole ride. My mind kept wandering back to last weekend, when Jameel had helped me study over pizza and popcorn. He'd made all these funny jokes out of the words on the vocab lists to help me remember them.

Maybe a break is a good idea, I thought. I slammed the book shut.

"Fine," I said. "I'll play."

"Great," Ronald said, smiling in that hyper-enthusiastic way of his. "So, let's go, who wants to start?"

"I'll do it," Salvador immediately volunteered. "But who's my first victim?"

Richard shrugged. "I'm up for it," he said.

Salvador grinned. "Truth or dare?"

"Dare," Richard responded right away.

"I dare you," Salvador began with a wicked gleam in his eyes, "to go up to the prettiest girl you see on this bus—from a different school," he added, with a quick glance next to him at Elizabeth. His crush on her was so incredibly obvious, it made *me* want to blush.

"Yeah?" Richard prompted. "Then what?"

"Tell her she looks *just* like your eighty-year-old uncle Roy," Salvador finished gleefully.

Richard frowned, but he stood and wandered toward the middle of the bus, stopping next to a couple of girls. They giggled at first when he leaned over to talk to them, but then as he spoke to the pretty redhead next to the aisle, her mouth dropped open and her eyes narrowed in fury. Richard hurried back to us.

"Okay, I need revenge," Richard told Salvador

as he slid back into his seat next to Bernadette. "Truth or dare?"

"Dare," Salvador answered.

Richard frowned in concentration, then a slow smile spread across his face. "The next truck that we pass," he said. "Moon the driver."

Elizabeth gasped. "What? That's not allowed!" she said.

"No problem," Salvador replied, like it was nothing. "Just one truck?" he asked, switching places with Elizabeth so that he was next to the window. "Are you sure? We could go for two. Or maybe three."

I rolled my eyes, glad that I wasn't sitting with him. Glancing at Elizabeth, I saw that her face was bright red.

"Just one," Richard replied with a grin. He leaned toward the window on our side of the bus and pointed. "That one there."

I saw a huge tractor trailer in the next lane. I kept my eyes on the trucker as Salvador—I assume—went through with the dare. The truck driver scowled in our direction, and Richard burst out laughing.

"Way to go, Butt-head!" Richard said with a chuckle as the tractor trailer sped up and left our bus in the dust.

"Can I look yet?" Elizabeth asked from behind her hands.

"Yeah, the boys are through being idiots," I reassured her.

She dropped her hands from her face and glared at Salvador.

"Okay, okay. My turn to ask again," Salvador said, ignoring the glare. He glanced around at each of us. His eyes glittered as his gaze lingered on me for a moment, and my palms started to sweat. I couldn't handle one of Salvador's questions. But then he glanced at Bernadette. "Bernadette," he said, drawing out her name as slowly as possible. "Truth or dare?"

Bernadette pressed her lips together anxiously, squirming in her seat. "Um, truth?" she squeaked after a moment's hesitation.

Salvador rubbed his chin thoughtfully. "Truth?" he mused. "All right. Here's your question. Please describe the underwear you're wearing right now."

Bernadette's cheeks turned bright red.

"That's not a *question*," I challenged Salvador. "It's obvious you're not competing in English, del Valle."

Salvador shrugged. "Okay, whatever," he said. "Bernadette, I will now present my question in the form of a question: What does your underwear look like? Please be as specific as possible." He grinned at me. "I mean, could you please be as specific as possible?"

I thought Bernadette was going to faint from embarrassment. But she cleared her throat and responded in a clear, though very quiet, voice. "Actually," she said, "they're light blue with white lace around the waist. And, um, they have candy canes printed on them. I got them last Christmas."

I glared at Salvador, daring him to laugh. But he didn't, and neither did any of the others, though I was pretty sure Richard was trying really hard not to smile. Salvador just shrugged. "All right, then," he said calmly. "It's your turn to pick someone, Berna."

Bernadette looked relieved. "Ronald," she said softly. "Truth or dare?"

"Hmmm." Ronald paused to think about it for, like, thirty seconds, as if it were some huge decision. I bit back a sigh, sneaking a quick peek at my watch. "All right," he said at last. "Truth!"

Bernadette nodded and smiled slightly. "Okay. Tell the truth—what was your best kiss ever?"

I laughed out loud, more than a little surprised at her question. I mean, this is a girl who's too shy to raise her hand if she has to go to the bathroom during class.

Ronald looked slightly sheepish. "Well," he said uncertainly.

"No cheating, Ronald." Salvador grinned and

wagged his finger under Ronald's nose. "We want the truth."

"Okay." Ronald blushed a really interesting shade of magenta. "The truth is, um, I've never really kissed anyone. A girl, I mean." He tilted his chin up slightly, like he was daring anyone to give him a hard time.

I glared at Salvador, who seemed to be on the verge of making some idiotic comment. *Leave him alone,* I thought. *Just drop it.* I really hate it when people tease someone just because they feel superior for some stupid reason.

Miraculously, Salvador didn't say anything about Ronald's admission. "Okay," he said with a shrug. "It's your turn, Ronald."

Ronald's whole body relaxed in relief. "Um . . ." He glanced around at all of us. Finally his gaze settled on Elizabeth. "Elizabeth. Truth or dare?"

"Gee, I wonder what she'll pick," Salvador teased.

Elizabeth stared at him defiantly, then gazed back at Ronald.

"Dare," she announced, crossing her arms over her chest.

Salvador's eyes widened in surprise, and even Ronald seemed taken off guard. Elizabeth's kind of a straight-arrow type, and it's not like her to do anything too wild. I scooted forward in my seat, finally taking more interest in the game.

"Uh . . . okay," Ronald said, nodding as an idea came to him. "I dare you to . . . bark like a dog!" He collapsed in laughter as soon as he'd said it. I caught Bernadette's eye across the aisle and exchanged a confused look. After the stuff Salvador and Richard had done, this was nothing.

Elizabeth took a deep breath and threw back her head, letting out a whole series of barks, yips, and even a long howl at the end. It was more risky than I'd presumed. Everyone on the bus stopped talking and turned to see what was going on. Even the bus driver was peering up into his rearview mirror, frowning in confusion. We all ducked down in our seats, giggling, until the attention passed.

This game wasn't so bad after all. I cast a glance at my Spanish book. *But I really should be studying,* I thought.

"Bethel," Elizabeth said. "Truth or dare?"

I blinked at the sound of my name.

"Oh," I said. "Uh, truth, I guess." No way was I going to risk having to do something embarrassing like fart in Ms. Upton's face or kiss the bus driver. Not that I thought Elizabeth would ask me to do anything like that. Then again, I never would have thought she'd do the Fido thing in front of thirty strangers either.

"Okay." Elizabeth gazed at me thoughtfully for a

second. "Here's your question: If you could be any-place in the world right now, where would you be?"

With Jameel. The answer flashed into my mind immediately.

I could feel my face growing hot. Where had that come from? I mean, yeah, Jameel's pretty cool, and he's fun to be around. So maybe we'd spent some time together lately. Okay, maybe, like, a *lot* of time.

"Whoa." Salvador was hanging over the back of his seat, watching me carefully. "Looks like this is going to be a good answer."

I flashed him an annoyed look. "Just a sec-ond," I muttered. "I'm still thinking."

"Yeah, right." He grinned. "Come on, Bethel. Give!"

I didn't know what to do. How could I admit what I was really thinking? When Elizabeth asked the question, she was probably expecting a normal answer, like that I wished I were accept-ing a gold medal at the Olympics or something.

I could say that, I told myself. But I'm a pretty bad liar. And the rules of the game are to answer with the truth, no matter what. One thing I've never been is a cheater.

"Okay," I said as calmly as I could, twisting my hands together in my lap. "Um, the truth is—I would be back in Sweet Valley hanging out with, uh, Jameel."

Salvador started making kissing noises, but he

stopped when Elizabeth elbowed him in the side.
Richard was grinning, and Elizabeth, Bernadette,
and Ronald were staring at me in curious surprise.

"You miss your *boyfriend*," Salvador teased.

"Jameel is not my boyfriend," I snapped. I bit
my lip as I thought about it—*was* Jameel my
boyfriend? No, that was ridiculous. Bethel McCoy
didn't need a boyfriend.

Then why did something kind of skip inside
me at the idea of being Jameel's girlfriend?

"Salvador," I said quickly. "Truth or dare?"

"Huh?" Salvador was rubbing his side and giving Elizabeth a wounded look. "Oh, um, dare."

"Okay." I racked my brain for something to
take everyone's mind off me and Jameel. "I dare
you to go up to the front of the bus, get down
on one knee, and beg Ms. Upton to marry you."

The others laughed, and Salvador grinned.
"You got it," he said, hopping out of his seat.

I couldn't hear anything from where were sitting, but I watched as Salvador dropped dramat-
ically to his knees and babbled at Ms. Upton for
a few seconds.

Luckily Ms. Upton was in a good mood. She
just rolled her eyes and told Salvador to go sit
down, probably guessing what he was up to. He
sauntered down the bus aisle toward us, wearing
a big, self-satisfied grin.

"She said yes," he announced as he climbed back onto his seat. "I'm irresistible."

"Bravo," I told him dryly. "Your turn."

"Oh yeah." He glanced around, his gaze settling on Elizabeth. "Wakefield," he said briskly. "Truth or dare?"

"I think I'll play it safe this time," Elizabeth joked. "Truth."

"Okay," Salvador responded with a sly smile. "I'm going to steal Berna's question. What was your best kiss ever?"

Elizabeth

For a second I was in total shock. How could Salvador ask me something like that—in front of everyone? The others were silent, staring at me curiously as they waited for my answer. I shot Salvador a quick glance. His dark eyes glittered eagerly.

I knew exactly what he wanted to hear. He expected me to describe one of the times *we'd* kissed. It had only happened twice, and both times *were* pretty amazing. Our first kiss was at a party Jessica and I threw at the beginning of the year. Salvador and I ended up alone in my brother's room. We'd sworn that would be the only time. But then Salvador and I were working on a story together for *Zone* one night at the top of the Sweet Valley Tower, this really romantic place. It was cold, and he put his jacket around me to keep me warm. We were looking down at Sweet Valley in the moonlight. And then . . .

I snapped myself out of the memory.

Kissing Salvador was great. *Really* great. But

the truth was, neither of those kisses was my absolute best kiss ever.

That would definitely be my very first kiss. It was with Todd Wilkins, who was my sort-of boyfriend for a while back at my old middle school. I remembered how nervous I was beforehand and how nice it felt when it happened. How it made me feel so close to Todd and so grown-up at the same time.

But how could I say that without hurting Salvador's feelings? I winced at his eager expression—he was definitely waiting for me to say that *he* was my best kiss ever. As annoyed as I was that he'd asked this question in the first place, I didn't want to hurt him.

"Um—uh . . . ," I stammered, trying desperately to think of a way out.

"Come on, Elizabeth," Bethel prompted. "Spit it out."

"Yeah," Salvador added. "It's a simple question."

I met his gaze, then flinched. "I'm thinking," I muttered.

A flash of hurt appeared in his eyes. Suddenly he didn't seem so excited to hear what I had to say. Ronald checked his watch, and Richard started humming the *Jeopardy* theme song.

Glancing at the others, I had an idea. "I don't think I should answer that question," I said. "I mean, it wasn't even original. You stole it from Bernadette."

Salvador's mouth kind of sagged at the corners. "So what?" he asked. "It's still a fair question."

"No, it's not," I argued. "No repeats."

"Says who?"

I shrugged. "I think I've heard that rule before," I said, moving my gaze away from Salvador's face. "I have to pass."

"Oh," he said flatly. "I see." He crossed his arms over his chest and turned around, plopping down into his seat. "It's a stupid game anyway. I don't feel like playing anymore."

"I agree," Bethel piped up. "This game is totally lame. And we all have studying to do for the contest." She reached for her books.

"Wait, does anyone want to play the license-plate game with me?" Ronald asked.

"Why don't we just hang out for a little while, no games?" Richard suggested.

Everyone settled back in their seats in silence. Salvador edged a couple of inches away from me and stared down at the floor.

"Look," I said after a few minutes of sitting next to a statue. "I'm sorry, okay? But it was really rude of you to ask me that as part of some stupid game."

"Why?" He finally faced me, his lips set in a

sullen pout. "It *should* have been a no-brainer." His eyes filled with hurt again. "At least, it would have been for me," he added quietly.

"That's not the point," I argued, feeling a lump rise in my throat at how sad he looked. "I don't want to talk about a *kiss* in front of all these people."

Salvador nodded slowly, then jerked up in the seat. "So answer now," he challenged. "No one's listening anymore."

I took a deep breath, then glanced away from him, out the window.

"Does this have something to do with that guy from your old school—what's his name again—Todd?"

I gulped but didn't say anything.

I'd almost forgotten that Salvador knew about Todd—they'd met at the party at my house.

"You *were* thinking about Todd, weren't you?" Salvador pushed.

"Please don't make a big deal out of this," I pleaded, fixing my gaze on him again. "I don't even talk to Todd anymore."

"Really?" Salvador asked. "Then why are you still thinking about kissing him?"

"I'm not—Salvador, this is ridiculous," I exclaimed in frustration.

He shrugged and picked at a loose thread on

the seat fabric, not meeting my eye. "It's just that I thought . . ."

"What?" I prompted. "You thought what?"

"I thought maybe—you know. That you *liked* kissing *me*."

I felt a blush creep back over my cheeks.

"I did," I admitted.

"Uh-huh." He scowled. "But I guess it was a lot more fun sucking face with good old *Todd*."

Okay, I understood why Salvador was hurt—but now he was just acting like a stubborn little brat.

"Look," I fumed, "I don't know what your problem is. It's not like you never kissed anyone else before—including your best friend, Anna!"

He actually jerked back a little, as if I'd slapped him.

"Fine," he snapped, his voice coming out kind of strangled. "Whatever."

"Yeah." I turned away and stared out the window, sick of the whole conversation. Sick of him. Sick of everything. "Whatever."

Salvador

I thought we would never get to Sacramento. Really. I was convinced that we were stuck in some kind of spatiotemporal-warp zone where we were all destined to spend eternity on a superfancy bus heading nowhere.

But finally, after just about a million and a half hours with only one stop at the most depressing rest area in the universe, we got off the highway and drove through the city streets of Sacramento toward the old part of town. I didn't see too much of the scenery since Elizabeth was still hogging the window seat and it was hard to get a good view around her big head. Eventually, though, we pulled up in front of the Stateside Hotel, which was a big, glass-and-steel building with tons of multicolored flags flying out in front.

"Okay, everyone," one of the chaperons from another school announced, standing up at the front of the bus. "We're here!"

A cheer went up from all over the bus.

"Yee-haw," I muttered.

"Please proceed off the bus in an orderly fash-ion," the chaperon went on. "Take your luggage with you into the hotel lobby. We'll show you where to gather while we get checked in— please don't wander off before we give you your room assignments."

"It's about time," I muttered, already standing up and reaching for my duffel bag. I didn't bother to look at any of the others as I hurried down the aisle, eager to take a breath of real fresh air.

Soon we were all crowding into the hotel's huge, carpeted lobby. There were tons of other kids our age already milling around inside. One of them, a tall, incredibly skinny guy with glasses and a bowl haircut, almost crashed into me as he wandered past, punching numbers into some supersonic-type calculator. A very pale girl with messy brown braids stood stock-still in the middle of the lobby, staring at the ceiling and muttering stuff like, "The year 1066—Battle of Hastings."

I rolled my eyes. Basically, the whole place was just what I'd expected—egghead city. Now that my chances of spending time with Elizabeth were blown, I realized I had *no* reason to be here.

"Hey," Richard said, walking up to me. "Pretty crazy scene, huh?"

"I guess," I mumbled. "Look, I'll be right back, okay? I'm going to find a soda machine."

Richard raised an eyebrow, smiling. "The chaperon said—"

"I'll be back before they even notice I'm gone," I cut in. I knew Ms. Upton and Mr. Martinez would freak if they saw me wandering around the hotel. But after that horrible bus trip I really needed some space. And some caffeine.

Heading across the lobby, I spotted a hallway leading off to the back near the elevators. A sign over it read Refreshments. "Bingo," I whispered under my breath.

Sure enough, the hallway led straight to a small snack bar. The counter was closed since it was the middle of the afternoon, but there were plenty of candy and soda machines lined up against one wall. I dug into my pocket and found a handful of change. I had just enough for a soda. A cola would perk me up. Carefully counting out the coins again to make sure I had enough, I dropped them into the slot one by one. Then I pressed the button.

Nothing happened.

I hit the coin-return lever. It made a sort of clanking sound, but none of my coins came out. Annoyed, I punched the button again.

Still nothing.

I tried a different button. Soda was soda, after all. But that one didn't work either.

Neither did any of the six others. Or the coin return when I tried it again.

I kicked the machine. Hard. So hard that my big toe went numb. I forgot I was wearing these dorky leather loafers instead of my usual sneakers.

"Ow!" I yelled, hopping up and down on one foot.

Suddenly I heard a giggle from behind me. Whirling around, my jaw almost dropped. I found myself staring right into these big, brown eyes the color of dark chocolate with long, long lashes. The eyes belonged to one of the best-looking girls I'd ever seen. Wavy, dark hair spilled over her shoulders, and her lips curved into a smile that suddenly made me want to grin like an idiot.

She was *gorgeous*.

"Uh—Uh, hi," I stammered, feeling like a total dork. A dork with a throbbing toe, I remembered as I felt another flash of pain.

"What's up?" the girl replied. Even her voice was amazing—sort of throaty and low but cheerful at the same time. She laughed. "Want a soda?"

I blinked at her. She was holding a can out to me.

"Uh, what?" I asked. God, was I running for dork of the year?

"You can have it," she said, taking a step closer and pushing the soda into my hand. "Obviously you're really thirsty," she added laughingly.

How long had she been standing there, watching

me? I started to blush like crazy. "Uh, thanks." I accepted the Coke, then just stood there for a second. *Pull yourself together,* I yelled in my head. "Thanks a lot. I owe you one. I'm Salvador, by the way."

"Erin Dunkerly." She was still smiling, so I guess she didn't think I was a total loser. "Are you here for the academic competition?"

"Uh-huh. Are you?"

"Yeah." She giggled. "Some kind of fluke of nature, I guess. Me and studying don't exactly mix."

"Same here," I said with enthusiasm. "I couldn't believe it when I found out I qualified for science."

She laughed again. Her laugh sounded so . . . free.

"I'm here for science too," she explained.

I popped open the soda and gulped down some, then offered it back to her. She took a few sips. "So where are you from?" I asked her.

"This tiny town called Smithfield. It's north of here. What about you?"

"Sweet Valley," I replied. "Near LA."

Coming to this geek convention was definitely having a negative effect on my social skills. I couldn't come up with a single funny thing to say.

Luckily she didn't seem to mind.

"So, Salvador," she began. She handed me back the Coke and then rested one slender hand on my arm. Her fingers were cool and slightly moist from the soda can. A jolt of happiness rushed through me. "What are you doing after the big dinner tonight?"

"Big dinner?" I asked lamely. "What big dinner?"

"Didn't you read the schedule?" she asked, her eyes twinkling with amusement. Elizabeth had thought I was some kind of jerk for not reading the schedule—but Erin just thought it was funny. "All of us are supposed to go sit around in the hotel dining room together and listen to speeches and stuff. I'm sure it will be totally boring."

I laughed. "Yeah, sounds like it."

"I figure after all that, I'll be dying to have some fun." She lifted her hand from my arm and ran her fingers through her thick, dark hair. "So do you want to hang out? We can check out the hotel—maybe even sneak out and see some sights."

I hesitated for a second, thinking about all the studying I hadn't done for the competition tomorrow. Then I glanced at Erin and almost smacked myself on the head. *What kind of lunatic would turn this girl down?* I wondered.

Not this one.

"I'm in," I told her, trying to sound as casual as she did. "Maybe we can even sneak out of the dinner early."

"Good idea," she agreed. "But just in case we don't hook up in the dining room, my room number is four-oh-one."

"Four-oh-one. Got it." I smiled at her, searching my mind for something witty to say. Instead I heard the faint sound of Ms. Upton calling my name from the direction of the lobby.

"Oops," I said. "I'd better go." Normally I wouldn't care about Ms. Upton's state of mind. But I didn't want to tick her off now. If she was watching me, it would be harder to sneak off and meet Erin.

"Okay." Erin gave me this cute little wave as I headed away and she sort of tossed her hair back over her shoulders. "Catch you later, Salvador."

"Yeah." I sighed happily as I strolled back to the lobby.

Suddenly this trip was looking up. *Way* up.

Bethel

"Stupid jerk," Elizabeth muttered under her breath as she rifled through her open suitcase. "How old is he anyway? I mean, really . . ."

I sighed and rolled my eyes at Bernadette as I passed her on the way to the closet. Bernadette smiled and shrugged in return. She was unpacking her suitcase into one of the dressers. The room was much nicer than what I'd expected. It was big and spotlessly clean, with two double beds plus a cot. I was relieved when I saw the cot. I have trouble sleeping when anyone else is in the same bed— once when my family rented this cabin in the mountains for a vacation, I had to share a bed with my older sister, Renee. I hardly slept all week. And this weekend I needed all the rest I could get to be in peak condition for the competition.

I opened the drawer in the bedside table to drop in my vitamins. Inside, along with the usual Bible and room-service menu, there was a post-card. I picked it up.

Stateside Hotel, it read in big, bold letters. Beneath the headline were three photographs—one of the hotel building, another of what had to be the hotel restaurant, and the third of a room almost identical to ours. The only difference was, in the photograph, instead of three tired eighth-grade girls, there was this goofy-looking family grinning their heads off and waving at the camera. They looked ridiculously, unbelievably happy, as if that hotel room were the best place they'd ever been in their lives.

It's hysterical, I thought, grinning back at the photo. *Jameel would laugh his butt off if he saw this!*

I grabbed a pen off the bedside table and scribbled Jameel's name and address on the right side of the postcard.

Hold it, I told myself, dropping the pen. *What am I doing? We're only going to be here for three days—Jameel might not even get the postcard before I'm back in Sweet Valley.*

Glancing over to make sure Elizabeth and Bernadette weren't paying attention, I quickly crumpled the postcard in my hand and tossed it in the wastebasket.

It freaked me out a little to realize how much I'd been thinking about Jameel already on this trip. I'm not used to thinking about someone this much. I've always been too busy focusing on stuff like running and school.

But then Jameel came along. And he made *no* secret of the fact that he was totally into me. It was pretty embarrassing at first—he's only in seventh grade, for one thing, which meant I heard a lot of stupid jokes about robbing the cradle. Plus it was weird to have someone just sort of *choose* me like that. Someone I'd never even noticed before. I wasn't sure I liked that feeling.

So basically, I spent so much time trying to get Jameel to stop liking me that I didn't even realize how much I was starting to like *him*.

After that, you'd think things would have gotten easier. But everything was still so weird. It was like running a really tough cross-country course for the first time. Challenging. Different. But sort of exhilarating at the same time.

Watching Elizabeth mutter and fume over whatever had happened with Salvador on the bus, I vowed never to get so obsessed with anyone. I mean, it was just sad. As I tossed my clean socks into a free drawer, I shot her another glance and saw that her fists were clenched at her side and there was a vein throbbing in her forehead. Literally throbbing.

"Look," I told her, unable to keep my thoughts to myself any longer. "Elizabeth, you have to calm down."

She spun around and stared at me. "What?"

I shoved the dresser drawer shut and tossed my empty bag in the corner. "It's a total waste of energy," I said. "Whatever Salvador said or did, it can't be that big a deal."

She frowned, then sank down onto one of the neatly made beds. "How do you know?" she asked.

I plopped down next to her on the bed, glancing over at Bernadette, who was still kneeling in front of the dresser, unpacking. She half turned and watched us with a curious expression.

"I mean, it's obvious that you and Salvador like each other."

Elizabeth's jaw dropped. "Wh-What?" she stammered. "Salvador and I are just friends. And right now, I don't even know if we're that much. Because after—"

"Just stop," I cut her off. "We all know you like the guy. So you fought about something. Fine. But here we are." I waved my hand around the room. "In Sacramento for the whole weekend. Wouldn't you rather just get over whatever's bugging you and have fun being with Salvador? I know if I could—" I stopped, not even believing what had been about to come out of my mouth. *If I could spend a weekend with Jameel . . . ,* I finished in my head, *I wouldn't let a silly fight get in the way.*

Elizabeth stared back at me thoughtfully, seeming not to notice that I'd stopped in the middle of a sentence. "You're right," she announced, standing up and surveying the room. "Salvador was acting pretty immature, but I can understand why he was hurt. I probably would have been too."

I jumped up and headed over to the dresser for my Spanish book.

"He really had no reason to be jealous," Elizabeth continued. "But maybe he didn't know that."

"Sure," I said, flipping through the pages of my textbook to find where I'd left off. "Just talk to him, and you'll both feel better. And then we can *all* get back to studying so we can blow those other schools away tomorrow, right?"

Bernadette stood up and looked at her watch. "Hey, it's almost time to go downstairs for the group dinner," she reminded us.

I checked my own watch and saw that she was right.

"Shoot," I muttered, annoyed at the waste of valuable study time.

Still, the chaperons had made it perfectly clear that everyone had to participate in all the events. So the three of us quickly changed out of our wrinkled bus clothes and into dressier outfits.

I was checking myself in the mirror to make

sure my blue sundress looked okay when Elizabeth came up behind me.

"Bethel," she said. "Thanks for what you said before."

"It's okay. I guess I can kind of relate," I said, grinning.

There I go again, thinking about Jameel. This had to stop.

Elizabeth

"That was pathetic," I said as Bethel, Bernadette, and I emerged from the hotel's tiny gift shop. "It's a good thing Jessica isn't here. She'd be mortally offended at the idea that you're actually supposed to *shop* there."

Bernadette giggled. "At least we got postcards, even though we'll probably already be home by the time our friends get them," she offered.

We all laughed at that. Pretty much the only souvenirs in the gift store were these silly post-cards with the words *Sacramento at Midnight* written at the top and then a black square where the city was supposed to be. They were pretty funny, so we bought a bunch.

"Come on, we'd better get to the dinner," Bethel urged, heading across the lobby to the banquet rooms. "I'm actually pretty hungry now anyway."

"Me too," I agreed. I'd been so mad at Salvador during the trip that I'd barely touched the turkey sandwich I'd brought along.

What a waste, I thought, shaking my head as I

61

quickened my pace to keep up with Bethel. *That fight was so stupid.*

I figured it was my fault as much as Salvador's. Yeah, he sort of freaked out about the kissing thing. But I could have been a little nicer. I knew I wouldn't want to hear about Salvador's best kiss—at least, not if it wasn't with me.

"Here's our dining room." Bethel pointed at a sign reading Statewide Academic Challenge, next to two large, open doors that led into a huge ballroom.

We stepped inside the room, and Bethel spotted Ms. Upton standing by a table in the middle of the room. Making our way between other tables, we headed that way. As we got closer, I could see that Richard and Ronald were already seated and Mr. Martinez was standing nearby, chatting with a teacher from another school. The place was already packed with students—it looked like we were among the last to arrive.

"Hi!" Ronald greeted us eagerly as we took our seats. I was careful to sit beside an empty chair since Salvador wasn't there yet. "Isn't this a great hotel? This trip is already so much fun!"

I couldn't help smiling at Ronald's enthusiasm. "It *is* fun," I agreed. "So what did you guys do before dinner?"

Ronald started chattering about unpacking and looking for the ice machine, but I wasn't really listening. I kept glancing over at the entrance, looking for Salvador. Now that I'd realized how silly it was to be fighting, I wanted to make up right away. I figured maybe after dinner we could walk around the hotel together or even take a walk outside if the chaperons said it was okay. That would be pretty romantic—an evening stroll in a new city, with a whole weekend ahead of us. . . .

"So what do you think, Elizabeth?" Ronald asked, breaking into my thoughts. "Richard and I were saying that all of us should have a study session after dinner. We could quiz one another and get focused for tomorrow."

Richard nodded. "Besides," he said with a smile, "we don't have to study the whole time. We can take breaks to hit the snack bar for brain food. So are you in?"

Ms. Upton chose that moment to find a seat at the table. Unfortunately, she chose the seat right next to me. Salvador's seat.

"Um . . . ," I began, but the teacher wasn't even looking at me. She was busy waving to somebody across the room. I sighed, giving up on the idea of making up with Salvador during dinner. But I wasn't ready to give up on my after-dinner plans. I leaned toward Richard and Ronald.

"You'd better count me out," I murmured, not

wanting Ms. Upton to overhear. "I think I might have other plans."

Richard shrugged, and Ronald frowned in disappointment. But Bethel gave me a little kick under the table, and Bernadette just smiled knowingly.

"By the way," I said, "do you guys know where, uh, where Salvador is?" I tried to keep my voice casual—according to Bethel "everyone" could tell what was up between me and Salvador, but I hoped that didn't include Richard and Ronald.

"He told us he'd meet us down here," Ronald said with a frown.

"Yeah, he kept trying on all these different outfits," Richard added, smirking. "Like he really cared how he looked or something. For a second I thought I was back home, watching my sister get ready for a date." He chuckled and shook his head.

"I think he just wanted to make a good impression on the judges," Ronald argued. "It could help for the competition tomorrow."

I bit back a smile. Salvador is *not* the kind of guy to care about clothes—or to worry about impressing a bunch of academic people. I had a feeling I knew why he was making such an effort to look good—probably the same reason I'd spent ten minutes choosing between wearing my hair back in clips or in a braid. He wanted to make up as much as I did. Still, I wished he would get here already.

Just then a tall, thin man strode over to the microphone set up on a little stage at the front of the room.

"Welcome, students!" he said once the room quieted down. "Welcome to the first annual Statewide Academic Challenge!"

A bunch of people cheered, including Ronald. I clapped lightly, but my gaze was fixed on the doorway. Where was Salvador? At the far end of the room I could see waiters and waitresses bringing out trays of food. The dinner was already starting—he was late.

"My name is Dr. Chester Trask," the speaker continued, "and I am in charge of this competition. Please allow me to introduce myself and the contest in more detail as you enjoy the delicious food our hosts are distributing at the moment." He gestured at the wait staff, then cleared his throat and continued. "I have been fascinated since boyhood by the quest for knowledge. . . ."

I did my best to pay attention, but the speech was pretty boring. Besides, I was still keeping a lookout for Salvador. It was obvious that our chaperons also noticed his absence. Ms. Upton was frowning and looking at her watch, while

Elizabeth

Mr. Martinez leaned over to ask the other two guys something. I was sure he was asking them where Salvador was.

A waiter in a tuxedo approached our table and began serving our dinners. I stared at the plates in amazement—I'd never seen such elaborate food. The vegetables were all arranged precisely on one half of the plate, and the chicken had some kind of sauce drizzled over it in a spiral design.

When the waiter put Bernadette's plate in front of her, she whispered something to him and he nodded and took it away, then replaced it with another plate from the tray behind him. Instead of chicken she got a pasta dish with her vegetables.

I guess Berna's a vegetarian, I thought. It was nice that they had meals for everyone. Salvador would have cracked another joke about the special treatment for eggheads or something. That is, if he had bothered to show up.

I glanced around the room for the millionth time, and this time I spotted Salvador. He was hurrying through the banquet-room doorway, looking around for the right table. Ms. Upton saw him too. She half rose out of her chair and waved until Salvador noticed her.

When he got closer, I decided that whatever had kept him up there for so long had definitely worked—he looked really great. His dark, wavy hair was sort of slicked back at the temples, and he wore a button-down shirt with a pair of dress pants. He always looked pretty cute, even when he was his usual messy self. But now he looked incredible. I smiled tentatively at him as he reached the table and slid into the empty seat beside Bethel, but I don't think he saw me.

I sat back in my chair and sighed. *Oh, well,* I thought. *I'll just have to wait a little longer to talk to him.*

But I didn't get a chance to talk to him for the rest of the meal. The speeches continued all through dinner. After Dr. Trask finally finished telling his life story, a couple of other contest officials got up and explained the rules of the competition. I tried to pay attention, but my gaze kept wandering back to Salvador. For once he wasn't goofing around. He just sat there with a little smile on his face, like he was thinking about something really great.

He's probably imagining all the fun we'll have once we make up, I thought.

As a waiter came to our table and started passing out bowls of sorbet for dessert, the last speaker finally wound things up by asking all of the chaperons to come forward for some last-minute instructions.

Free at last! I thought with relief as people

started chatting with one another. Mr. Martinez and Ms. Upton got up and hurried toward the front of the room. *Now's my chance.*

I pushed back my chair and started to get up to go talk to Salvador. At that moment I noticed a girl approaching our table. She was really pretty, with long, wavy dark hair, and she smiled as she came toward us. I smiled back at her. But the smile froze on my face as she stopped behind Salvador's chair and put her hand on his shoulder.

"Hey, Sal," she greeted him. "Ready to explore?"

I couldn't seem to stop staring at her hand, which was still resting on his shoulder. Her fingernails were cut short and painted bright blue. My own fingers tightened around my spoon as I glanced around the table. Ronald was engrossed in noisily slurping down his sorbet. Richard and Bernadette appeared curious. Bethel was watching me but looked away as soon as I caught her gaze.

"Hey, Salvador," Bethel said bluntly. "Who's your new friend?"

Salvador's cheeks turned pink. "Oh," he said, shooting me a quick glance before looking around at the others. "This is Erin. She's here for science too, like me."

I felt a little twist in my stomach.

"Yeah," Erin spoke up with a smile. "Sal

and I met by a soda machine earlier. He still owes me a soda."

Salvador laughed really hard, as if Erin had actually said something funny, which she hadn't.

"So are you still up for our plans?" Erin asked, fixing her gaze back on Salvador.

Their *plans?* I struggled not to wince.

"Definitely." Salvador hopped up from his chair. "Let's bail." He grabbed Erin's hand, and they quickly scurried away, weaving through the crowd and then escaping out of the ballroom. Still holding hands.

Ronald finally looked up from his dessert long enough to notice what was happening. "Uh-oh," he said, sounding worried. "I don't think they're supposed to leave before we're dismissed."

I frowned. "Yeah, well, that's the chaperons' problem, not ours," I snapped.

I blinked back tears of hurt. While I'd been agonizing over my fight with Salvador, he'd been off making new friends. Cute, bubbly new friends with bouncy hair and blue fingernails. He didn't care if we made up or not—he didn't care about me at all!

"So about that study session," I said, jabbing viciously at my sorbet. "What time do you guys want to start?"

Jessica

"Perfect," I whispered, smiling at my reflection in the mirror on Friday night. I twisted and turned, taking in every angle of my favorite lavender cropped T, paired with Elizabeth's new black capri pants. Since she wasn't home to wear them herself, I figured she wouldn't mind if I borrowed them.

My stomach fluttered as I headed downstairs to drag Steven away from some stupid ball game to drive me to Damon's. I always got nervous like this before seeing Damon—and now that we were practically a couple, it was just more intense than ever.

Steven dropped me off at the curb in front of Damon's trailer and then roared away, nearly breaking the sound barrier as he raced back to his exciting evening in front of the TV.

Taking a deep breath, I headed across the tiny scrap of lawn toward the front door. I reached up and pushed the buzzer.

Damon's the first person I've known who lives

in a trailer instead of a house or an apartment, and at first I was kind of weirded out. It is pretty small, but it still feels like a home. It's nice.

"Hey," Damon greeted me when he opened the door. His eyes traveled quickly up and down, and he smiled. "Wow. You look really good."

"Thanks."

Damon looked great too, as always. He wore a black T-shirt with dark blue jeans, and his eyes looked bluer than ever.

I walked inside as he held open the door for me. His little sisters, Kaia and Sally, sat on the floor of the main room, coloring on some construction paper.

"Jessica!" Kaia exclaimed when she saw me. The two girls dropped their markers and ran over, each hugging one of my legs.

I laughed. "Did you miss me?" I asked them. A few weeks ago I baby-sat for Damon's sisters all by myself. It was a pretty crazy morning, but I made it through okay. And they *were* sweet kids.

Damon smiled. "Okay, you two," he said in this mock-stern voice. "Remember what we talked about. You got to say hello to Jessica, so now you're going to go play in your room until bedtime. Right?"

"Okay," Sally said. She let go of my leg and pulled her little sister off the other. "Damon wants to be lonely with Jessica," she said.

Damon started to blush, and I let out a giggle. Then both girls raced down the short hallway leading to their bedroom in the back end of the trailer, giggling wildly.

"My mom left a little while ago," Damon told me as I set my purse down on a small end table and perched on the couch. He walked back to the door and opened it, glancing outside before pulling it shut again. "Uh, I don't know if I mentioned it, but she's out on a date."

"Yeah, you said something about that," I told him. "So what do you want to do?" I glanced over at their small TV. "Want to watch something?" I suggested.

Damon peeked at his watch with a worried frown.

"I'm sure there's something decent on," I said.

"Huh?" He stared at me, confused. "Oh, uh, no. It's not that. I was just—well, I realized my mom never said what time she'd be home."

"Oh." I held back a smile. Damon wanted to be alone with me for as long as possible. The feeling was definitely mutual.

Damon walked over to the TV set and switched it on, adjusting the antenna until a picture emerged. He flipped the channels to a sitcom I'd seen a few times, then joined me on the couch.

"This all right?" he asked, gesturing at the television.

"It's great," I said, relieved. I scooted a few inches closer to him until our elbows were almost touching. "I love this show. But I almost never get to watch it at home because my brother's always watching sports."

Damon laughed. "My sisters get on my case if I watch the hockey game when their favorite cartoons are on."

At the first commercial break Damon got up and brought us sodas and pretzels from the kitchen area. Then he sat down next to me again, so close that our legs were almost touching. It felt so great just being there with him. Hanging out, like a real couple.

Then, as the commercials ended and the show came back on, I noticed him peering at his watch again. He did it twice more in the next few minutes.

"Hey." I poked him on the shoulder. "Do the girls have a strict bedtime you're afraid to miss?"

Damon chuckled, but his forehead was still all crinkled, like he was concerned about something.

"Sorry," he said. "I was thinking that my mom and her—uh, date—are probably at the restaurant by now. So I was just trying to figure out how long it'll take them to eat."

"Oh."

Why is he freaking out about when his mom gets home? I wondered. I mean, yeah, it's a pretty small trailer. It wasn't like we could sneak down to the basement and kiss. But it was still early, and besides, he hadn't even tried to put his arm around me yet or anything.

"Uh, Damon?" I asked cautiously.

He glanced at his watch again. I nearly screamed.

"I really wish she had told me when she'd be home," he muttered.

Wait a second here, I thought. *Is he hoping his mom will stay out late—or get home early?*

Maybe he kept checking his watch because he was counting the seconds until it was time for me to leave!

I frowned. "Look," I said, irritation building up inside me. "If you and your watch want to be alone, I can call my brother to come pick me up right now."

"No!" He put a hand on my arm. "Please, Jessica. Don't go. I'm really glad you're here." He stared into my eyes, his gaze sweet and sincere.

"Are you sure?"

"Definitely." He moved his hand down my arm and then wound his fingers around mine.

I held my breath, wondering if he was going to kiss me. My heart started to race at the idea.

But he didn't.

Instead he let go of my hand and draped his arm around me, then leaned back against the scratchy couch cushion.

Oh well, I thought, snuggling against him. *I guess he probably doesn't want to seem pushy.* After all, Damon and I *still* hadn't shared a full-on kiss yet, even though we'd been sort of talking for a while now.

We sat that way for a few minutes, cuddled together. Damon even seemed to get into the show—laughing a few times at the jokes. But then it happened again . . . I caught him shifting his left arm slightly so he could see his watch. A slight frown crossed his face, and he glanced toward the front door with that same worried crease between his eyebrows.

I scowled in frustration. It's not like I needed Damon to bow down and worship me or anything.

But it would have been nice if he even remembered that I was in the room.

Salvador

"Salvador? Earth to Sal. You there?"

"Huh?" I blinked and snapped out of my thoughts. Erin gazed at me with her big eyes and waved a hand in front of my face.

"Oh. Sorry," I told her, shaking myself as I glanced around the empty hotel hallway. "I was, uh, just thinking about something." I tried to push away the image of the hurt expression in Elizabeth's eyes when she saw me with Erin. It wasn't like she'd cared when she hurt *me* earlier.

"That's your first mistake," Erin teased. She laughed. "Thinking too much. Gets you in trouble every time."

"Can I quote you on that?" I joked. "I'm always getting in trouble with my teachers because they say I don't think *enough*."

"No prob. Now come on—let's check out the game room. I think it's this way."

She grabbed my hand and took off down the hall.

"So what games do you like?" I asked Erin as I

followed her. "I happen to be a total pinball master," I bragged. "But I also play a mean Ping-Pong."

Erin just laughed. "Here we are," she said, gesturing at a doorway in front of us.

We entered the game room, and I took a look around. It was big—almost as big as the arcade at the Red Bird Mall. Video games lined one wall, and a couple of little kids were standing in front of the Tetris machine, squealing and fighting over the controls. The center of the room was taken up with a few pool tables and an air-hockey table. Only one of the pool tables was being used—by a couple who looked like they were probably the parents of the brats playing Tetris.

"Pretty decent for a hotel," Erin commented. "Check it out—air hockey."

"Air hockey rules," I agreed. "Want to play?"

Erin shook her head. "First I want to see if you can live up to your title."

I tilted my head in confusion. "Huh?"

She pointed across the room, and I spotted a couple of pinball machines in the corner.

"Prepare to be amazed," I said, rubbing my hands together eagerly. I shot Erin a cocky grin. "Think you can take me on?"

"Is that a challenge?" Erin's eyes sparkled with interest.

I shrugged. "Maybe."

"Good. You're on!"

We raced over to the pinball machines and dropped our quarters in the slots. I relaxed as soon as I started to play, enjoying the quick pace of the action.

Erin was actually pretty good—she lasted much longer than Anna usually does. She didn't even complain when my turns took forever because I kept getting extra balls.

"Yes!" I shouted, pumping both fists in the air after I won what had to be my millionth free game. "I am the supreme pinball champion of the universe!"

Erin giggled. "I bow before you," she said. She bent down in front of me, causing her long hair to fall over her face when she stood back up. I had to restrain myself from reaching out to brush a few strands away from her eyes.

"How'd you get to be so good anyway?" she asked.

"Many years of intense study," I replied, faking a serious tone. I started to blush, worried that I would seem like a loser for spending so much time in arcades. "So do you want to play anything else?" I asked quickly.

Erin shrugged. "We don't have to stick around here."

I blinked, wondering what else she had in mind. It was getting late—what if Mr. Martinez found out I wasn't in my room? I could only hope Richard and Ronald would cover for me— pretend I was in the shower or something if Mr. Martinez stopped by to do a bed check. I wasn't worried about Richard. He seemed pretty cool. Ronald, on the other hand . . .

"Hey." I nudged Erin as she leaned forward to watch someone at the pool table try a tough shot. "We should probably get out of here."

"Yeah, this is getting old," she agreed. "Let's see what else this place has to offer."

I guess she's not worried about getting in trouble with her chaperons, I thought. *Unless she doesn't care because she just can't get enough of my irresistible personality and sparkling wit.*

That made it pretty hard to think about teachers and room checks.

Still, as we wandered out of the game room, I couldn't help but worry about the next day's competition.

"I was thinking," I said hesitantly. "Maybe we should go do some last-minute studying. You know, for tomorrow."

She rolled her eyes. "I thought we both *agreed* that studying is lame," she said. "I heard there's an indoor pool here somewhere. Why don't we go find it?"

I stared at her uneasily, torn between my desire

to follow Erin absolutely anywhere and guilt over the competition.

"Sal, why waste our time studying when there's so much fun stuff to do here?" Erin prodded. "Right?"

I did ace the science-aptitude test without cracking open a book, I thought. So maybe I didn't need to study for tomorrow either.

"Right," I finally said, nodding. I glanced around the hall, which was completely empty except for the two of us.

"We're here in this totally amazing hotel," Erin continued. She stepped closer to me, near enough that I could smell her shampoo—some kind of really pretty flower scent. "No parents. No chaperons in sight. What could be better?"

She had a point. "Not much," I said. I'm used to being the goof-off, the king of irresponsibility. It was nice to finally meet someone who made *me* feel like a total straightedge.

"So are you ready for a little swim?" she asked, tossing her hair back behind her shoulder.

I grinned. "I'm there," I said, feeling a rush of excitement.

My heart raced as Erin and I snuck back through the lobby. Even though none of our teachers was around and the rest of the hotel guests probably didn't know we weren't supposed to be there, it was fun to act like secret spies, hiding behind plants and statues when we heard people nearby.

Finally we found the indoor pool in a big, glassed-in courtyard on the other side of the tennis courts. The bright blue water sparkled under the electric lights. Nobody else was there, so we took off our shoes and socks and dangled our feet in the water.

Erin pointed at a big sign on the wall near the entrance. "So what do you think?" she asked. "How many of those are we breaking?"

I scanned the sign.

POOL RULES
1. Swimsuits must be worn in pool area.
2. Guests are not allowed in the pool unless lifeguard is on duty.
3. No running in pool area.
4. No horseplay.
5. Children under age eighteen must be accompanied by parents.
6. Swim at own risk.
7. Hotel not responsible for lost or stolen items.

"I don't know," I told her, shaking my head. "We've done number one, two, and five already. Should we go for . . . number four?" I slid one foot through the water and splashed Erin's legs, which were bare below the knees, where her loose, flowered skirt ended. She shrieked and splashed me back with both feet, soaking my dress pants.

"No fair," I complained. "Your clothes are still dry." I kicked the water with more force and created a big wet spot on Erin's skirt.

Her jaw dropped in mock outrage, but I could see the laughter in her eyes. She leaned over and scooped some water up in her hands. Before I could dodge away, she dumped it over my head.

"Hey!" I jumped to my feet, then tossed my head, sending water droplets flying from my hair. "You'll pay for that!"

She hopped up. "You have to catch me first!" She raced away toward the kiddie pool.

"Wait!" I yelled, taking off after her. "You're breaking rule number three—no running in pool area!"

"Okay," she shouted back. "Then I'll just run *in* the pool!"

She stepped into the kiddie pool, which was only about a foot deep, and splashed through it. I followed, not even caring that my pants were getting completely drenched. I finally caught up to her next to the lifeguard's stand.

"Truce!" she cried, laughing as she hoisted herself up to the ledge. She pushed a few wet strands of hair back behind her ears.

I grinned and pulled myself up next to her. I couldn't imagine doing something like this with Anna or even Elizabeth. They would have been so mad if I'd gotten their clothes wet, but Erin was wringing out the end of her skirt and giggling like it was nothing.

"Are you cold?" I asked her. My legs were kind of chilly through my dripping pants.

She shook her head. "I don't get cold easily," she explained, smoothing out her skirt. "At least, not around here. I lived in Boston until I was about eight."

"Really?" I stretched my legs out in front of me. "Why'd you move to California?"

"Actually, I didn't. I mean, not at first. We lived in Texas for a while, then Colorado, and then we came to California."

"Wow," I said, staring at her in disbelief. "How come you moved so much?"

"My stepdad's in the navy," Erin explained with a frown. "He and my mom got together when my mom and I were in Boston. Ever since, our family never stays anywhere for too long."

"That's so weird—my parents are in the army," I said. It was amazing how much Erin and I had in common. "But I live with my grandmother, the Doña, because my parents travel all over the world."

83

Erin cocked her head, and her big, brown eyes looked thoughtful, more serious than they had all day. "I never thought of doing that," she said. "You know, staying with someone besides my mom. I don't really mind all the moving. At least, not anymore. I've kind of gotten used to it, and it's fun to see new places. And . . . meet new people," she added. She gave me a wink, and I felt my cheeks start to burn as I realized she meant *me*. "Do you miss your parents a lot?" she asked, her expression solemn again.

I chuckled. Recently my parents had come for a visit, and it was a big reminder of the way my dad and I are *not* from the same apple tree or whatever that expression is. Still, we kind of have an understanding. I think.

"Sometimes I do," I admitted. "My mom, especially. My dad and I . . . we're pretty different. But the Doña's a really cool grandmother. She's not like most grandparents. She's always taking classes and learning new stuff, like dancing or fencing or tai chi."

Erin giggled. "She sounds pretty wild," she said.

I smiled. "Definitely. But she's also . . . Well, she cares about me a lot." I stopped, realizing that I was saying stuff to Erin that I never say to *anyone*—even my best friend, Anna, or Elizabeth. Talking to Erin was just so easy. I wanted to stay there with her all night.

Wait, what time was it anyway?

I glanced up at the clock on the wall and saw that it was eleven—*way* past curfew. I scrambled to my feet.

"We should go," I said nervously, holding out my hand to Erin. She took it, and I helped her up. "I'll walk you to your room."

"Thanks," Erin said, brushing off the back of her skirt. "I think we'd better be careful," she warned as we walked together toward the exit. "Can you imagine what our chaperons would say if they saw us like this?"

I started to laugh as I checked out the soggy bottom of Erin's skirt and my own damp pants.

Luckily we reached her room without running into anyone. When we got there, Erin tipped up her head and smiled at me.

"Thanks, Sal," she said softly. Her voice made my heart pound faster. "That was fun."

"Yeah," I said, suddenly as shy as I was when I first met her. I wanted to kiss her. Boy, did I want to kiss her. But I had no clue if she wanted me to. How could I find out? What if I—

"Good night," she whispered. Then she quickly slipped open her door and disappeared into the room.

"Good night," I said to the door. I stuffed my

hands in my pockets and headed back to the elevator.

As I pushed the button, I stood there imagining how adorable Erin had looked with the water dripping from her wet strands of hair and the way she had watched me so closely when I talked about my family.

I stuck my hands back in my pockets, and my fingers brushed up against a crumpled piece of paper. Pulling it out, I saw it was the schedule for my events the next day.

I never studied, I realized as the elevator arrived with a little ding noise. *Oh, well,* I thought as I stepped in and pushed the button for my floor. *Maybe I can get in a little review time tomorrow morning.*

Damon

It was like the time Sally hid the TV antenna and we could only get one station. My mind was totally tuned in to one channel—my mom's date.

That would have been fine, if I were sitting home alone.

But Jessica Wakefield—*my* Jessica—the girl I liked so much and had asked over, was sitting right next to me. And she was obviously getting seriously annoyed with me.

"Uh, listen," I told Jessica, shifting on the sofa to face her. Her expression was stone cold. "Sorry I'm so out of it tonight."

"Whatever," she said with a frown. "You know, maybe I should—"

"Damon!" Sally appeared in the doorway, yawning. "Kaia fell asleep on Mommy's bed."

I winced as I realized I'd totally forgotten about the girls. Jessica and I had been watching TV for almost an hour already, which meant it was way past their bedtime.

I jumped to my feet. "Sorry, Sally. I'll be right there. Why don't you go put your pj's on, okay?"

Sally nodded sleepily and went back toward the bedrooms. But she turned just before she reached the door of the little room she shared with Kaia.

"Jessica," she mumbled. "Will you come tuck me in?"

Jessica hesitated and glanced at me. Then she smiled at Sally. "Sure," she told my sister brightly. "Go get changed, and I'll be right in."

"Thanks," I said to Jessica as Sally disappeared into her room. "She really likes you."

Jessica shrugged. "Come on, let's go put them to bed."

I followed her back to my sisters' room, wondering if she was mad. Soon we had the girls tucked in, and we returned to the main room. As I headed for the fridge to get us more soda, I vowed to focus on my own date from now on instead of on my mom's. "So what should we watch now?" I asked.

Jessica was leaning over the TV set, flipping through the channels. "How about this?" she asked, stopping and taking a step back to reveal an old Audrey Hepburn movie that had just started. "I've always wanted to see this. The clothes are so cool."

"Sounds great," I agreed, returning to my spot on the couch.

Jessica got settled next to me, and I tried to focus my attention on the screen. It was pretty hard to concentrate, though, when I couldn't stop my brain from obsessing over how close we were sitting on the couch. Were our hipbones three inches apart? Two? And her arm—did it actually brush mine when she reached for her soda, or was it just the breeze the motion made tickling the hairs on my own arm and giving me goose bumps?

Suddenly a very unsettling thought occurred to me. Was that guy—Ben—thinking the same kinds of thoughts as he sat with my mom in the movie theater?

I jerked forward a little at the idea, and Jessica gave me a sidelong glance.

"What's wrong?" she demanded. "Are you bored?"

"Uh . . . I just got a shiver," I explained.

"Huh." She inched away from me and folded her arms over her chest. I didn't blame her. I was acting like a freak.

We watched about a half hour of the movie in total silence. Every time I shifted around or glanced at my watch, Jessica let out this little sigh. The tension was unbearable.

Suddenly I heard a key turning in the lock of the door. A second later my mother walked into the trailer, followed by this tall, lanky guy with a full, brown beard and round glasses. Once I saw him I recognized him—I *had* seen him around the diner a couple of times, I realized now. They were both laughing at something as they stepped inside, and I stiffened at the sound.

"Damon," my mom greeted me in this light, breathless voice. "Hi, sweetie. Hi, Jessica."

"Hello," Jessica said politely.

"This is Ben." She linked arms with bearded guy, pulling him forward. "Ben Jarrett, this is Jessica. And you remember my son, Damon."

"Hey there, Damon." Ben's voice was friendly. "Good to see you again." He smiled at me, his eyes twinkling like a younger Santa Claus's.

"Hmmm," I replied, checking him out carefully and trying to rate his smile on the sincerity meter. Hard to gauge.

"Well, it's getting late," Ben said cheerfully. "I'd better hit the road." He looked back at my mother, and I followed his gaze, noticing that her whole face was just really *bright*. "So we're still on for tomorrow, right?"

"Absolutely." Mom smiled as Ben leaned down and gave her a quick kiss on the cheek. I wanted to pull him off her, but I knew that would be slightly psychotic. He gave me and Jessica a quick wave good-bye, then left.

"Tomorrow?" I blurted out as soon as the door closed behind Ben. "What's tomorrow?"

"Saturday?" She laughed as if that were the funniest thing she'd ever said. Then I guess she realized I wasn't too amused, so she stopped laughing. "I invited Ben over here for dinner tomorrow night."

"Oh." Two nights in a row? Was it me, or was that moving way too fast? I glanced at Jessica. Her face was set in a calm, normal-looking smile, like there was nothing weird about my mom's whirlwind romance.

"So what did you kids do tonight?" my mom asked, setting her purse on the little table by the door. "Did you have fun?"

"We just watched TV," Jessica said. She shrugged and looked at me, frowning slightly.

"That's nice." My mom smiled at her, then glanced over at me. "I hope the reception wasn't too bad tonight. Our antenna is pretty old."

"Uh, it was fine," I muttered. I really wanted to ask her more about her date with Ben, but I didn't want Jessica to think I was a total freak.

"Oh, good, I'm glad you had a nice time."

"Yeah," Jessica said quietly. I glimpsed a hint of disappointment in her pretty, blue-green eyes. "My dad's coming to get me soon."

My heart sank. The night had been a disaster—Jessica'd had a terrible time, and I was too big of an idiot to make her feel better.

A horn honked, and Jessica jumped up from the couch.

"It's probably my dad," she said, grabbing her purse and rushing over to open the door. Sure enough, Mr. Wakefield was waiting in his car. "Okay, then," Jessica said, not meeting my gaze. "I'd better be going. Good-bye, Mrs. Ross. See you Monday, Damon."

I hardly had time to say "bye" before she was gone. I watched her walk to her dad's car, noticing the way the moonlight made her light blond hair shine in the darkness. How had I managed to mess this night up so badly?

When I turned around, my mom was puttering in the kitchen area, pouring herself a glass of juice.

"So," she said brightly. "What did you think of Ben? Do you remember him now?"

I shrugged. "Sort of," I said. "He seemed okay, I guess."

"Good. I'm glad you think so. I think he's pretty okay too." She sounded giddy, like Sally does when we give her some toy she's been asking for forever.

Okay enough to get serious with? I wondered. But I was afraid to ask the question out loud.

I didn't want to hear the answer.

Sacramento at Midnight

Yo, Anna,

   As you can see from the incredibly
detailed and colorful picture on the
front of this card, Sacramento is
a pretty thrilling place. But the good
news is I haven't been arrested
yet or anything.

   Anyway, to sum up my trip so
far: The weather's here, wish you
were beautiful. (Ha ha!) Just kidding.

                    Love,
                    Salvador

Elizabeth

I woke up very early Saturday morning to the sound of loud knocking.

"Jess?" I called, sitting up in bed and rubbing my eyes. When I opened them, I was staring directly at unfamiliar, paisley wallpaper.

Then it came back to me. I wasn't in my bedroom in Sweet Valley.

"What's going on?" a soft voice mumbled. I turned and saw Bernadette lying on the cot next to my bed.

"Who's there?" I called.

"It's Ms. Upton," she responded from right outside our door. "Our team is meeting in the hotel coffee shop for breakfast in forty-five minutes. I expect to see you all there."

Bernadette and I hopped up immediately, and I stumbled toward the bathroom to start getting ready. Bethel stood and stretched up her arms, letting out a big yawn.

"You two go ahead," Bethel said. "I think I'll stay here and do a little more studying."

"Bethel!" I protested, looking at her in the mirror over the dresser as I brushed my hair. "You can't skip breakfast—you need energy to help you think. Besides, you studied like crazy last night. I'm sure you're totally prepared."

Bethel frowned, her eyebrows knit together tightly. "But I never got around to going over those irregular verbs," she muttered, taking a step toward her books, which she'd stacked neatly on the table beside her bed. "All I need is another half hour. . . ."

"No way," I told her. "You have to come to breakfast. Ms. Upton said she expects to see *all* of us." I paused. "Think of it as sort of a pep rally."

Bethel rolled her eyes, but a small smile crept over her face. "Yeah, right," she said. "An academic pep rally?"

"Why not?" Bernadette piped up. She was carefully applying eyebrow pencil to her thin, wispy brows. Dropping the pencil on the dresser, she did an awkward little leap. "Go, team!"

Bethel and I laughed.

"Okay, okay," Bethel said. "I'll go. As long as Berna promises *not* to go out for cheerleading next year!"

Berna giggled, and then we all went back to getting ready.

It took Bernadette about ten minutes to find

her shoes—one was under the bed, and the other was jammed behind a suitcase in the closet—so by the time we headed downstairs, Richard and Ronald were already sitting in a booth in the coffee shop with juice and cereal in front of them. Ms. Upton and Mr. Martinez were at a smaller table nearby, sipping coffee.

Where's Salvador? I wondered uneasily.

"Hey, teammates," Bethel greeted the guys, sliding into the booth beside Ronald. "Everybody ready to go out there and win today?"

Bernadette squeezed in after her, so I took the seat next to Richard.

"I hope we're ready," I joked. "We studied so long last night that I think I fractured my brain."

Bethel grinned. Then she seemed to notice that Salvador wasn't there.

"Hey, so where's your roomie?" she asked the guys.

They exchanged a glance. "He's up in the room, doing some last-minute cramming," Richard said.

"Yeah," Ronald added. "He was, um, out pretty late last night."

Bethel snorted. "See?" she said. "That's where I should be right now. Studying."

I hardly heard her. I could feel my face turning red. Salvador was "out pretty late"? How late? Was he with Erin?

So much for trying to make up and have fun together

this weekend, I thought angrily. *I guess Salvador decided he'd rather just have fun with someone else.*

I caught Richard glancing at me out of the corner of his eye. But he turned away quickly, smiling across the table at the others.

"Hey," he said brightly. "When do you guys have lunch today? Maybe we could meet up somewhere. Like somewhere outside the hotel."

He was obviously trying to change the subject. I felt a flash of gratitude. *He's a really nice guy,* I thought. *Unlike some other guys . . .*

After checking our schedules, we discovered that half the competitors had their lunch break at noon, while the other half had to wait until one o'clock. Math, foreign languages, and geography had the early lunch, and the other three subjects got the late one. That meant Richard was the only one at the table with the same lunch break as me. *Hmmm.*

While Bethel, Bernadette, and Ronald made plans to meet up, Richard faced me, flashing his cute, crooked grin. "So I guess it's just you and me," he said.

Yeah, since Salvador will probably spend his lunch drooling over Erin, I thought.

"Why don't we just meet in the lobby after our morning rounds?" I suggested. "Then we can decide where to go." Unlike with dinner, we were allowed to leave the hotel for lunch.

"Sounds great," Richard agreed, sipping his juice.

Yeah, great, I thought halfheartedly. That wasn't *exactly* the word I'd use to describe any part of this weekend, but I still hoped things would get better. They couldn't get much worse.

Salvador

"The next question is for Salvador del Valle," the judge announced from his podium. "Mr. del Valle, please tell me what an atomic number is and its primary purpose."

I blinked.

I knew this, or at least I knew it at one time. But my mind felt sluggish and slow, like it wasn't quite running at full power. The fact that I'd had less than five hours of sleep probably had something to do with it.

I shot a quick glance around the hotel meeting room that was being used for the science competition. All the contestants sat at two long tables on either side of a stage set up in the center. The judge's podium loomed high on the stage, and a few spectators were seated on folding chairs in front of us.

"Um . . ." I willed myself to focus on the question, but I just couldn't form an answer in my head.

"An atomic number—uh—is slang for a really slamming dance tune?"

I grinned weakly as a few people tittered. The judge glared at me sternly over his bifocals.

"I'm sorry, but that's incorrect." He didn't sound very sorry, if you asked me. "The question goes to Erin Dunkerly. Ms. Dunkerly, would you like me to repeat the question?"

"That's okay—I've got it," Erin said, leaning forward in her chair and narrowing her eyes thoughtfully. She was sitting directly across the stage from me, about thirty feet away, looking just as chipper and alert this morning as she had the night before. Her hair was pulled back on the sides in cute little barrettes, and there wasn't a single bag under her pretty brown eyes. If I didn't know better, I would think she'd had at least ten hours of sleep. So far, she hadn't missed a single question. "An atomic number is the number of protons in an atom. Scientists use it to tell different elements apart."

"Correct." The judge smiled at Erin approvingly, and she sat back in her seat.

Just my luck—thanks to the fact that the judge went in alphabetical order, Erin had corrected every wrong answer I'd given. She probably thought I was a complete idiot by now.

I don't get how she's doing so well, I thought. Erin had studied as little as I had. She must be really smart—either that or a really good guesser.

As the judge read the question to the next

contestant, Erin slowly twisted her head in my direction and caught my eye. She winked and flashed me a grin, and I smiled back, my worries instantly fading.

Who cared about some stupid science competition anyway? Even if I didn't get a single question right for the rest of the day, it had been worth it to hang out with Erin. I couldn't wait until the morning's round was over so we could get lunch together. If I wasn't one hundred percent positive that Ms. Upton and Mr. Martinez would strangle me, I would be tempted to talk Erin into skipping the afternoon session and going to the zoo or someplace fun.

I was picturing the two of us walking by the lion's den and maybe sharing an ice cream cone when I realized that the judge had said my name.

"Mr. del Valle," he repeated. My head snapped up, and I saw the glint of annoyance in his eyes. He shuffled his cards. "Your next question. Please tell me the formula for determining an object's density."

"Density," I echoed. I knew this. But the answer seemed to hover somewhere just out of reach. "Density," I said again, stalling for time. "Um, the formula for density . . ."

"Yes, Mr. del Valle?" the judge prompted with a frown. Talk about impatient!

"Density," I said one more time. I gulped and took a stab. "Uh, force per unit area?" I knew that wasn't right, but it was the only formula I could think of because I'd studied it just that morning.

"No." The judge didn't even pretend to be sorry this time. "Ms. Dunkerly, your question. *Again.*"

"You find density by dividing an object's mass by its volume," Erin responded confidently.

Duh, I thought, feeling a flash of irritation with myself. *I totally knew that. I'd better get a clue here, or they'll kick me out of the competition for having a negative score. Then I won't have any excuse to sit here and look at Erin. . . .*

The kid sitting next to me nudged me under the table, jolting me out of my thoughts. For a second I was about to shove him back, but then I realized he was handing me a folded slip of paper. I took it and unfolded it in my lap so the judges couldn't see.

HEY, SAL,
    TOUGH LUCK ON THE LAST QUESTION.
BUT DON'T WORRY—I STILL DON'T THINK
YOU'RE "DENSE." ;-)
    CAN'T WAIT FOR LUNCH. SEE YA THEN!

ERIN

I could feel myself grinning like a dork as I read the note over two or three times. When I glanced up, Erin was watching me. I waved at her behind my rule book, hoping the obnoxious judge didn't notice.

Okay, so maybe I was totally blowing this round. But so what? I didn't want some stupid, geeky academic prize anyway. Especially when the alternative was having a great time with an awesome girl like Erin.

Damon

"Jessica?" I clutched the phone tighter and leaned against the kitchen counter. "Uh, hi. It's Damon."

"Hey," she replied. "How's it going?"

I hesitated, trying to figure out from her voice if she was still mad about our messed-up date last night. It was kind of hard to tell—she sounded as upbeat as always.

"Um, it's going," I replied, glancing over at the bathroom door. My mom was taking a shower. A really long shower. "So I was wondering—if you're not doing anything tonight, how about if we go see a movie? That new one everyone's talking about just opened over at the Red Bird Mall."

I held my breath, waiting for her answer. I definitely wasn't in the mood to hang around the trailer for Mom's dinner with Ben, even though the girls were going to eat with them and they'd invited me too. I wasn't exactly ready to do the whole family-dinner-with-a-stranger thing. Besides, I really didn't want to blow my chance with

Jessica, and I had a feeling I would if I didn't fix things soon.

"Tonight?" she asked. "Okay, I guess we could do that."

I let out a relieved sigh.

"Cool," I said. "There's a seven o'clock show. Let's say we meet in front of the theater at quarter of?"

"Sounds fine to me," Jessica replied.

My mom floated into the kitchen in her bathrobe, her hair wrapped in a damp towel, smelling like the lavender shower gel I'd given her for her last birthday.

"Okay," I said quickly into the phone. "I'll see you then, Jess."

"Great. Bye, Damon." She sounded genuinely happy, which made *me* happy.

"So," I said to my mom after I hung up the phone. "Since the girls are going to be with you, I thought I'd go out with Jessica tonight. Is that okay?"

"Sure, sweetie." She hummed as she started digging around in the cabinets, pulling out pots and pans and ingredients.

I glanced at my watch. It was barely one o'clock. "You're cooking already?" I joked weakly. "When were you planning to eat dinner, three?"

She laughed. "Don't be silly," she said cheerfully. "I'm just getting an early start. I want everything to be ready so I don't have to be in the kitchen when Ben gets here."

"Oh." I felt my jaw tighten. "I'm going to get in the shower now that it's free," I told her.

When I got out of from the bathroom about twenty minutes later, I could hear my mom talking to someone on the phone as I towel dried my hair. At first I assumed it was Ben, so I tried not to listen.

But I started to tune in when I realized that her voice sounded upset.

". . . and I've already started cooking!" I heard her exclaim as I walked into the room. "I just can't . . ."

She paused and listened for a moment.

"Everything okay?" I mouthed, but she waved her hand at me to be quiet.

"All right," she said at last. "I'll call my friend and postpone." She sighed. "I'll be there by five."

She hung up and sighed again. Her shoulders drooped, and her eyes looked *so* sad. I can't stand seeing my mom like that.

"Who was that?" I asked, slinging the damp towel over my shoulder as I stepped closer to her.

"It was my boss." She leaned over and peeked into the oven, then switched it off. "Two of the other waitresses just called in sick, so he needs me to come in."

"But Saturday's your day off."

She shrugged. "Not this Saturday," she muttered. Then she gasped and put a hand on my arm. "Oh no! But I can't ask you to baby-sit tonight—you already made plans with Jessica."

My heart sank. "That's okay," I said. "I'm sure she'll understand."

Yeah, right, I thought. *She'll understand that I'm blowing her off at the last minute.*

"Wait, I have an idea," my mom said, her brow creased in a thoughtful expression. Picking up the phone, she quickly punched in a number.

"Who are you calling?" I asked. We don't know that many people in California yet, so it wasn't like she had a whole list of alternate baby-sitters. I just hoped she wasn't calling her boss back to say she couldn't make it—I didn't want her to get in trouble with him because of me.

"Hello, Ben?" she said into the phone. I cheered up a little as I realized that at least this meant Ben wouldn't come over after all. "It's Cheryl. I'm afraid there's been a slight change in plans. . . ."

I listened as she explained the problem at work. *Oh well,* I thought. *Maybe I won't get to go out tonight. But Mom and Ben won't get to have their big romantic dinner either.*

". . . so anyway," Mom was saying, "since Sally and Kaia are so crazy about you, I'm sure they'd be fine with it."

Wait a minute. What had I just missed?

She paused to listen to whatever Ben was saying on the other end. Then she laughed.

"I'll try not to be jealous," she said in a light, teasing voice. "It's okay if you like my daughters better than me. As long as you're willing to baby-sit on no notice, that is."

Baby-sit? I couldn't believe it.

"Mom," I hissed, tugging at her sleeve. "What are you doing?"

She ignored me. "Okay, then, we'll see you at four-thirty," she said. "Thanks again, Ben. And thanks for understanding about dinner too. We'll make it up, I promise. Bye." She hung up the phone.

I stared at her, my hands on my hips. "What was that all about?" I demanded. "Don't tell me you're actually planning to let Ben baby-sit Kaia and Sally!"

She rolled her eyes and smiled. "What's wrong with that? The girls have met him at the diner a bunch of times, and they think he's great. He likes them too—he's wonderful with kids. He watches Betty's kids all the time."

"But . . ." I didn't know how to convince her. It was bad enough my mom was getting all attached to Ben, but if my sisters did and then he turned out to be a bad guy . . .

"Besides," she went on, "this works out well for all of us. Ben and the girls can get to know one another better, maybe watch some TV together, and you still get to go to the movies like you planned."

I hesitated, remembering the cold expression on Jessica's face when she left my place the night before. It *was* pretty important that I make everything up to her.

"Well," I said slowly, "I guess if you really think it will be okay. . . ."

"It will be fine," she assured me. She picked up a pot of water that had been boiling on the stove and dumped it into the sink. "I guess Ben can just order pizza."

Already Ben was bringing over a big cheese pie to share with my sisters in front of the TV. It sounded like a perfect family moment—except that Ben *wasn't* part of this family.

Was he?

Bethel

"The next question is for Bethel McCoy, competing in Spanish," the judge began in her clear, high-pitched voice.

I sat up straighter, feeling my body tense up the way it does right before a race.

"*Por favor, describa lo que es un buen día para Usted, incluyendo detalles como; cual es la hora favorita del día, las cosas que le gustan hacer y las personas con las cuales se encuentra.*"

My throat suddenly felt very dry and scratchy. I swallowed, trying to process what the judge had said and figure out my answer.

A typical fun day for me. Let's see, what do I like to do? I like to run. I like to talk to Jameel and hang out with Jameel. . . . No, stop thinking about Jameel.

I took a deep breath, then glanced around at the other competitors. My eyes landed on a guy at the end of my row, and I blinked.

Jameel?

No, it couldn't be—Jameel wouldn't be here.

110

The judge cleared her throat. "Ms. McCoy?" she prompted.

But he looked *so much* like Jameel. I couldn't believe it.

"*¿Me puede repetir la pregunta?*"

Well, his hair was a little shorter, and maybe his lips were kind of fuller, but from a distance he could easily be mistaken for . . .

"*¿Tiene algún problema?*" the judge asked loudly.

I jumped. *Get it together,* I told myself.

"No, *perdoname,*" I said quickly. "*Tengo, mmm . . . un buen día . . . me levanto y hace mucho calor, voy a la nevera y saco un delicioso Jameel—*"

"Excuse me?" the judge interrupted in English.

Oh my God, I thought, wincing. *Juice! I drink a delicious glass of* juice—*not a delicious glass of Jameel!*

I blushed, noticing in amazement how the Jameel look-alike even *smiled* sort of how Jameel does.

"If you would like to pass, we can move on to the next contestant," the judge told me, peering at me intently.

I sank down in my chair in embarrassment. This was *not* going well.

Elizabeth

"The morning session is now officially over," the judge announced. She smiled at all of us. "Good work, everyone. We will resume the competition later this afternoon."

I stretched my legs out in front of me, realizing that I'd been sitting for a while. Our last juice break had been quite a long time ago.

My stomach grumbled as I pushed back my chair.

I guess I'm hungry, I thought. I'd only picked at my eggs at breakfast, and although I'd fought hard to stay focused on the tough literature questions, thoughts of Salvador kept pushing their way into my head. What was he *doing?*

I strolled out of the room and headed for the hotel lobby to meet Richard for lunch.

Well, I bombed pretty badly, I thought, flinching at the memory of telling the judge that the "what's in a name" speech is from *Macbeth.* Not only have I read *Romeo and Juliet,* I've even seen the movie like five times.

But we're just getting started, I told myself. *I need to get used to the format, and then I'll be able to concentrate better on the questions. Then maybe I—*

I stopped as soon as I entered the lobby, my hands tightening into fists at my sides. Right across from me, near the elevators, was a little cluster of chairs and sofas. Most of them were empty—the lobby wasn't very crowded—but one of the sofas was occupied.

Salvador and Erin sat next to each other, with barely any space between them. He was tickling her, and she was shrieking and trying to keep her long, wavy hair out of her face as she defended herself.

I blinked, feeling tears collect in my eyes.

I can't believe this, I thought. *A day ago we were on the bus together and he was tickling me. And now . . .*

Suddenly I realized how idiotic I must look, standing there gaping at the two of them. Luckily they hadn't spotted me yet.

I took a deep breath, glancing at the hotel's entrance. I spotted Richard standing near the revolving glass door. He was waiting for me.

With a sigh of relief I hurried over to him.

"Hey, Richard," I said.

He spun around, and his face broke into a wide grin. At least *someone* was happy to see me.

"Hey," he greeted me. "How did it go?"

"Not too great," I replied honestly. "It's so

depressing. I thought I was so prepared, but the questions were much harder than I expected." I shrugged. "They didn't tell us our scores or anything, but I don't think I'm doing better than about fifteenth place so far."

"Fifteenth place?" Richard rolled his eyes and grimaced. "I'd kill for that. I totally choked when the judges started asking about the Louisiana Purchase. And after that, I was so mad at myself that I messed up a bunch of really easy questions."

That made me feel a little better. At least I wasn't single-handedly ruining our team's chances for a group medal.

"Should we go find someplace to eat?" I asked. "I'm starved!"

"Me too," Richard said. "Hey, during one of our breaks this morning I was talking to this kid who lives here in Sacramento. He said there's a really cool burger place near here. Want to check it out?"

"Sounds great," I said. "Let's go."

We waited a few seconds while a group of people went through the revolving door ahead of us.

"I hate these things," I said. "They make me so nervous."

"So we'll go together," Richard offered. The next time there was an opening, he took my hand and pulled me in with him, pushing the door so it kept revolving. He held on to my hand until I was safe and sound on the other side.

Out on the sidewalk Richard peered down the street.

"Huh," he muttered under his breath. "I'm not sure if he said left or right."

The door swung open again behind us, and I heard people laughing. I felt my chest tighten as I recognized the guy's laugh.

"I know, that judge was such a weirdo," I heard Salvador say. The girl he was with— Erin?—giggled loudly. I refused to turn around.

Was he *following* me or something? What if he *did* see me watching him with Erin in the lobby and he dragged her outside with him just to rub it in my face how happy they were together?

If he's trying to make me jealous, it won't work, I swore to myself. It *wasn't* working.

"Let's try this way," I said, and began walking quickly down the street. Richard shrugged and followed me.

Luckily it was the right direction. I mean, *any* direction that took me away from Salvador and Erin was the right one, but the burger place ended up being just around the corner. Richard and I walked inside and got in line for a table. The restaurant was decorated like a fifties diner, with old records playing on the jukebox. I even recognized a few of the songs from my dad's collection

115

and started to hum along as we waited.

When we moved up to the front of the line, some goofy Elvis Presley song came on that my dad plays all the time. I mouthed the words to Richard, pretending like I was singing the song to him. He started laughing, and I stopped.

"Hey, don't stop," he said. "You know, you're pretty cool, Wakefield," he continued. "I didn't think you were like this."

"Really?" I smiled at him. "Why, what did you think I was like?"

Richard shrugged. "I don't know," he said. "All I really knew was that you're smart, and you seemed pretty serious. But you're a wild and crazy gal," he joked. "And you're pretty too."

I blushed, suddenly feeling awkward. Richard was staring at me with this weird look in his eyes, like he was totally focused on me. Even though it made me nervous, I didn't glance away.

"Thanks," I said shyly.

The hostess, wearing a wide, pleated skirt and saddle shoes, came over and brought us to a booth in the back that happened to be near the jukebox.

Richard pulled some quarters out of his pocket before he sat down. "I'll buy you a soda," he said, "if you promise to sing along to any song I pick."

I giggled. "Like, sing out loud?" I asked.

Richard nodded. "*Really* loud. Think of it as an extra dare from our game on the bus," he said.

I frowned for a second as I thought about how that truth-or-dare game had messed things up for me and Salvador.

Then I glanced up at Richard again, directly into his eyes, which looked dark green right now against his green T-shirt. His warm, friendly smile brought a grin back to my face.

"Go for it," I told him, waving my hand at the jukebox. "But I'd prefer a milk shake," I added with a giggle. "Vanilla."

Sacramento at Midnight

Dear Jessica,

Well, this trip isn't exactly what I was expecting. I'm writing this as I sit on a bench in the state capitol building. It's actually kind of impressive—lots of marble floors and sparkly chandeliers. We're waiting for the tour guide to find another tour guide who speaks Swedish—there's this couple from Stockholm who kind of barged their way in on our tour—so it could be a while.

Meanwhile I'm just sitting here, thinking how people are always surprising each other. I've sure found out some new things about a few people on this trip. Including someone I hardly knew before but also someone that I thought I knew pretty well . . .

Oops! Our guide's back. I'll tell you more when I get home. Bye!

Love,
Elizabeth

Bethel

"Salvador," I hissed sharply. "You have got to chill. Or I'm going to have to kill you."

Salvador stopped shifting from foot to foot. He also stopped humming. That was good because he was totally off-key.

"Sorry, Officer McCoy," he whispered.

I sighed and rolled my eyes. I definitely wasn't in the mood to deal with Salvador right now. Not after my pathetic first day in the competition.

Ever since our group had arrived at the capitol for the tour, Salvador had been acting like a total freak. Of course, Elizabeth wasn't exactly being Ms. Normal either. I flashed a glance at her as our tour guide blathered on and on about the capitol rotunda, how it was built in the nineteenth century and was over a hundred feet high.

Elizabeth didn't seem too impressed. She stood near the back of our group, which consisted of the six of us plus the two chaperons and this weird couple from Sweden who just sort of walked up and joined us. It was completely obvious that Elizabeth wasn't listening to a word the guide said. She just stared blankly at the high dome of the rotunda. Her expression didn't even change when the guide switched over to Swedish to repeat what he'd just said.

Beside me I could feel Salvador starting to jump around again. When he crashed into me and almost knocked me into the Swedish woman, I ducked behind Ronald.

I glared at Salvador as I rubbed my arm where he slammed into me. He didn't notice because he was too busy sneaking glances at Elizabeth. She didn't notice his glance because she was still staring at the ceiling, obviously ignoring him. I scowled at both of them. They didn't notice that either. *I don't know what their deal is, but they're totally out of control! It just goes to show how liking someone can get you in trouble. . . .*

I pushed that thought out of my mind quickly and tuned back in to the tour guide, who was speaking English again as we moved slowly across the marble floor.

Finally, after we'd listened to the complete history of the capitol building, Ms. Upton and Mr. Martinez told us we could go out to the capitol gardens and wander around for a while before heading back to the hotel for dinner.

The six of us started down one of the manicured

paths, Ronald in front with Bernadette and then the rest of us following.

"So," Ronald said brightly, turning his head so we could hear him. "How did everyone do today?"

I felt like growling at him, but I kept quiet. It wasn't Ronald's fault that I was messing things up for myself—and for the team. It certainly wasn't his fault that the kid sitting in my row looked exactly like Jameel. Or that I couldn't seem to stop staring at him—not even when the judge was asking me a question.

That was my fault and mine alone.

"Not too great," I said, trying to sound matter-of-fact. "I'm in, um, thirty-seventh place right now."

"Whoa." Richard, strolling along next to me, shook his head. "Sorry. I'm not doing much better, though—twenty-third place." He shrugged. "Who knew there was so much to know about the Great Depression? I mean, it's kind of depressing, you know?"

That got a laugh out of the others, and I forced myself to smile along. But inside, I was still furious with myself.

Thirty-seventh place. Out of forty!

I glared at an innocent rosebush as we passed by. Thirty-seventh place. *That* was depressing. And all because I couldn't keep my mind on the game.

"So?" Richard prompted. "Bethel and I gave it up. How are you guys doing?"

"Well," Ronald admitted over his shoulder, "actually, I'm in second place right now. But the girl who's winning is only one point ahead of me." He shook his head sadly. "If only I could have remembered that the internal angles of a *hex*agon are one hundred and twenty degrees and in a *hep*tagon they're one twenty-eight point six."

We were all silent for a second, and I glimpsed Salvador holding back a huge snort.

"Still, second place. That's great, Ronald," Elizabeth finally said. "Good for you."

"Yeah, good for you," Salvador mimicked without looking at Elizabeth.

Ronald smiled, but I could feel the fire radiating from Elizabeth.

"Well?" Richard looked at Bernadette's back. "Hey, Bern—how about you? Are you as embarrassed as the rest of us?"

Berna turned and blushed. "Um, sort of," she practically whispered. "I'm in sixteenth place. I should have done better," she added quickly.

"No, that's great!" Elizabeth told her sincerely. "I missed, like, the last four questions in a row. I ended up in nineteenth place."

She glanced down at the dirt path, shaking her head, and I knew exactly how she felt. I

knew how they all felt—like they'd let themselves down. Because that was how I felt too.

Suddenly I realized that one of us hadn't fessed
up yet. I peered around Richard at Salvador.

"Spill it, del Valle," I ordered. "How are you doing?"

Salvador shrugged and grinned. "Let's just say
I'm upholding my lifelong reputation," he said.
He pumped a fist in the air. "Yesss! Second-to-last
place!"

Our chance for a group award was definitely
shot. And it wasn't all my fault. We were failing mis-
erably as a team. It was a team *non*effort. Pathetic.

"You know," Elizabeth said coldly, addressing
Richard, "I think it's a shame when people don't
take this kind of thing seriously, don't you?" She
pursed her lips. "I mean, it kind of ruins things
for the whole team when *certain members* goof
off and do poorly."

Richard stared back at Elizabeth in surprise,
and Bernadette suddenly seemed very interested
in examining her fingernails.

I felt a flash of irritation. I knew Elizabeth was
just trying to hurt Salvador because she was
mad at him, but she made it sound like anyone
who hadn't done as well as Ronald was pur-
posely messing things up for everyone.

"Give me a break, Wakefield," I snapped.
"Nobody here has the right to be annoyed.

Except for maybe Ronald," I added with a glance in his direction.

Elizabeth's eyebrows shot up. "I wasn't talking about you, Bethel," she said quickly. "I mean, I was just making a comment. That's all."

"Uh-huh." I folded my arms across my chest. "Well, you can keep your obnoxious comments to yourself."

She frowned. "I just think we all need to work harder," she argued. "And some of us need to work even harder than others."

"Hey, people," Salvador said, holding up his hands. "Come on, now. Can't we all just get along?"

"Shut up!" I shouted, sidestepping to avoid trampling a little patch of roses. "You're the whole reason we're having this conversation. If you weren't such a goof-off, maybe the team would be in better shape."

Salvador snorted. "Oh yeah?" he said. "Is that so, Ms. Thirty-seventh Place?"

"Look." Elizabeth jumped in before I could let loose on Salvador. "This isn't getting us anywhere. Obviously all of us—" She shot a look at Ronald. "Well, most of us are disappointed with our standing. But there's still another day of competition. So why don't we do something constructive about this? We can all get together tonight and study. We'll quiz one another."

"Sure," Richard began. "That sounds—"

"Forget it," I interrupted him. No way was I going to sit around quizzing Ronald on algebraic equations or helping Bernadette memorize the capitals of Europe. I could get a lot more done on my own. Maybe even enough to bring up my score tomorrow. Elizabeth was right about one thing—the competition wasn't over yet. "I'm going to study by myself tonight."

Elizabeth frowned, but she didn't protest. "Fine. What about the rest of you?"

"I'm sorry, Elizabeth," Ronald said tentatively. "Uh, I already have plans tonight. A bunch of kids from the math competition are going to the planetarium."

"I don't think I can make it either," Bernadette said. "I have to go to bed early tonight. I need sleep more than I need studying."

Salvador shrugged. "For anyone who's interested, I definitely won't be there," he said, staring at a spot in the air somewhere over Elizabeth's left shoulder. "I have better things to do." He turned and stomped off down the path.

Elizabeth frowned as she watched him go. Then she shrugged. "Whatever," she said, her voice cold. She turned to face Richard. "So, Richard, I guess it's just you and me."

Salvador

How is it that I never noticed what
a snob Elizabeth can be? I wondered as I made my
way across the lobby toward the ballroom for
tonight's group dinner. I still couldn't believe the
way she'd acted in the garden today, like she was
so superior or something.

"Hey," a soft voice called out from behind
me. I whirled around and spotted Erin in black
jeans and a striped shirt, *not* exactly appropri-
ate dress for the banquet hall. She looked
much more comfortable than I felt in my
starched, button-down shirt and dress pants. I
stared at her.

"What are you—"

"Shhh," she interrupted. She grabbed my
arm. "Do you really want to sit through another one of those boring things?" she asked
as she pulled me in the direction of the hotel
entrance.

"What do you mean?" I asked, glancing back
over my shoulder as I followed her. Other kids,

dressed to make their parents and teachers proud, filed by on their way to the ballroom. But no one seemed to be watching us.

"I mean let's get out of here," she said, her eyes bright with excitement. "I saw this cool diner down the street today. Wouldn't you much rather have a big, juicy burger than another one of those fancy chicken things?"

I laughed. "Well, yeah, but—"

"But what?" she demanded. "Sal, I thought you were up for adventure."

Of course I was—what was wrong with me? And the last thing I wanted was to disappoint Erin.

I grinned. "Let's go."

We hurried outside and then ran down the street, even though no one was chasing us.

"This is it," Erin said, stopping in front of the restaurant.

I paused to catch my breath, then glanced down at my outfit.

"I think I'm a little overdressed for this place," I said awkwardly.

Erin checked me out, moving her eyes up my outfit and then letting her gaze linger on my face. She smiled.

"You look great," she said sincerely. "Come on." She took my hand and pulled me inside.

I surveyed the funky, fifties-style decor

around us, barely even noticing much. I was too busy glowing over Erin's compliment.

I'm used to hearing stuff like, "Salvador, you're so much fun," or, "Salvador, you're so funny." But girls never say anything about how I *look*. And to hear someone as beautiful as Erin actually say something like that . . .

Wow.

"So what do you think?" Erin asked as we got in line.

I gave her a wide smile. "I think we're . . . *it's* perfect."

Jessica

I slumped down in my seat in the movie theater and frowned as Damon shifted and glanced over his shoulder for about the millionth time.

What was his problem anyway? I was starting to get a serious complex. Okay, the movie wasn't exactly the greatest thing I've ever seen. But we were on a date, away from everyone. Just us, finally.

Unless that's the problem, I wondered uneasily. What if Damon didn't *like* being alone with me? What if he didn't like *me* at all?

Maybe he just needs to go to the bathroom, I thought hopefully. *And he doesn't want to leave my side.*

But when the credits started to roll, Damon grabbed my hand and dragged me out the side door of the theater—right past the rest rooms in the mall aisle outside.

"Hey!" I protested, yanking my hand out of his. "Why are you in such a rush?"

"Sorry," he said, glancing back at me. "Uh, I

just thought we'd head back to my place. I mean, it's late."

I bit my lip. It was just after nine. Was he really that eager to ditch me?

"I'm kind of hungry. What if we grab something to eat at the food court?" I suggested. Actually, I had zero appetite. But I was testing him to see how he'd react.

"I can't," he blurted out. He gulped, his forehead creased in worry. "I mean, I really should get home and check on my sisters." He paused. "We have food there. You can come back with me. If you want to, I mean."

It was obvious that Damon was only inviting me because he was too nice to just admit the truth—what he *really* wanted was to get rid of me.

"I think I'm going to go home, actually," I said through clenched teeth. I tossed my hair back over my shoulder.

Damon's shoulders drooped, and his frown deepened. He was doing a pretty good job of faking disappointment.

He touched my arm. "Jessica, I'm really sorry," he said softly. "I know I'm acting kind of weird. I don't want to mess things up. You know, with us."

I lifted my chin. "Really? Because it feels like

that's exactly what you're trying to do," I said without thinking. I winced as soon as the words came out of my mouth. Then I whirled around and headed toward the pay phones to call my brother to come pick me up.

"Jessica . . . ," Damon called after me.

My heart gave a little twist to hear how sad his voice sounded, but I willed myself to keep walking.

I was sure Damon was it, I thought.

But it looked like I was way wrong about that.

Elizabeth

I stretched my arms over my head and let out a big yawn. "Wow," I said, checking my watch. "It's after ten."

"Ready to take a break?" Richard pushed his history textbook away. "We could go for a walk or something."

I'd been thinking more along the lines of heading for bed. But a walk with Richard sounded like a nice idea. Something about him was just . . . I don't know. I liked being around him.

"Sure," I said. "Let's go."

We were sitting in a corner of the lounge near the hotel lobby, so we gathered up our books and stacked them next to a chair where we could pick them up later. Then we headed out a side door into the large courtyard between the hotel and the building next door.

It was dark, with just a few old-fashioned lanterns adding to the light of the moon. We strolled around the courtyard for a few minutes without speaking.

I sighed as I thought about my lousy performance earlier today.

"What's wrong?" Richard asked.

I shrugged, feeling silly for obsessing over the competition. I was starting to remind myself of Bethel, and *that* was scary.

"I was just remembering all the questions I missed today," I admitted. "I can't stop thinking about this one on Dickens I got wrong. I totally knew it—I just couldn't remember the stupid name."

Richard smiled sympathetically. "Yeah, I messed up on some stuff I knew too. It's hard with all the pressure, though. Don't keep beating yourself up."

I cringed. "Or everyone else either," I added.

He frowned. "What do you mean?"

"Oh, come on, you don't have to be nice," I said, hugging my arms around myself as a light wind blew through the garden. "Bethel was right—I did act like a jerk at the capitol today."

"You were just stressed," Richard argued. "It's totally understandable." He glanced at my arms, which had broken out in goose bumps. "Are you cold?" he asked.

I started to shake my head, and then another breeze came and I shivered. Richard laughed.

"Here," he said, shrugging off his corduroy jacket. "Take it." He draped it around my shoulders. The material was soft, and it felt nice and warm on my skin.

"Thanks," I said. "And thanks for saying I wasn't out of line today with everyone at the capitol—even though I still think I was."

Richard ran a hand through his brown hair, pushing a few strands away that the wind blew in front of his face. It was hard not to feel my pulse quicken a little as I thought about how good he looked in the moonlight.

"You're probably going to think I'm a complete dork," I began, "but I kind of thought I actually had a chance to win this competition. It's not like I always have to be the best or anything; it's just that I feel like I haven't even really tried. I'm mad at myself."

"I know what you mean." Richard stared at the ground as he walked, kicking idly at a clump of dirt on the grass. He shoved his hands into his pockets. "It's like how I am about my grades. I *know* I can do well. And if I don't, I feel like I've let myself down. So why wouldn't I do my best and get straight A's if I can?"

I stared at him, amazed to hear my own thoughts echoed by someone who seemed so, I don't know, *cool*.

"Exactly," I agreed. We stopped walking and

stood next to each other under a big oak tree, both of us quiet.

Richard took a few steps toward me, looking down into my eyes. My breath caught as I held his gaze.

I shivered again, but this time there wasn't a breeze. His face started to inch closer to mine, and I gulped, feeling my heart pound like crazy.

Then the side door of the hotel banged open and a big group of people spilled out into the courtyard.

I giggled nervously. "Maybe we should get back inside," I said, blushing.

Richard smiled and shrugged. "Sure, okay," he agreed.

We wove through the crowd of people and headed into the hotel, stopping in the lounge to pick up our books.

Whoa, I thought as we walked to the elevators together. I was almost positive that Richard had been about to kiss me!

While we waited for the elevator, I snuck a peek at Richard. His face was perfectly calm, like nothing weird was going on at all. My hands felt clammy, and I brushed them against the sides of my jeans.

The elevator arrived, and we stepped inside.

"Why don't you come up to our room?" I

asked as I pushed the button for my floor. Immediately my cheeks flamed up in embarrassment. "I mean, because Bethel will probably be there," I added hastily. "And I wanted to apologize to her, for today. I mean, if you're not ready to go to bed yet—um, we could all hang out."

Richard just grinned at me. "Sounds fine," he said. "Maybe we can order ice cream from room service or something."

"Yeah, maybe," I replied, beginning to relax. Whatever had been about to happen out in the courtyard—if anything really *was* about to happen—was just some weird moonlight thing or maybe even a figment of my imagination.

Richard was cute, smart, fun, and easy to talk to. But I did *not* have a crush on him.

Salvador

"You know what?" I told Erin as we left the ice cream parlor where we'd shared a giant banana split. Erin had insisted that we get our dessert somewhere besides the diner where we ate so that we could see as many different places as possible. "I'm glad you convinced me to ditch that lame dinner at the hotel."

Erin smiled. "Do you think anyone missed us?" she asked.

An image of Elizabeth flashed through my head, but I quickly pushed it away. It was weird—even though I still felt bad about fighting with her, I didn't really *miss* her the way I thought I would. I was having so much fun with Erin that it was hard to think about anyone else.

"Doubt it," I finally answered. "So what's next?"

Erin plumped her lips into a pout. She was so cute. "You're not worried about getting back to your room to study or anything?" she teased.

Luckily it was too dark outside for her to see the blush that rose to my cheeks. How could I,

Salvador del Valle, have actually considered cutting short my last night with Erin because of a pointless academic competition?

"I don't *need* to study," I joked, puffing out my chest as we strolled down the street. "Didn't you notice how brilliant I was today?" I rolled my eyes. "Tell me the truth—you think I'm a complete idiot, don't you?"

Erin reached out and took my hands in hers, squeezing my fingers. "I think it's cool that you're not taking the whole thing megaseriously," she replied. "And some of your answers were really funny, although I don't think the judge thought so."

I laughed giddily, my temperature rising about thirty degrees as Erin wound her fingers more tightly around mine.

"I'm here to amuse," I said.

Erin stopped walking, and she stared up at me, frowning slightly.

"What's wrong?" I asked.

"I don't want you to think that's all you are—someone who just makes people laugh."

"What do you mean?" I asked self-consciously. I couldn't stop blushing.

A small smile passed over Erin's lips, but her eyes remained serious. "You're a really smart guy, Salvador," she said quietly. "You're not a clown. There's a lot more to you than your jokes." She shrugged. "I just wanted you to know that, that's all."

I swallowed, watching the way the light wind blew wisps of her dark hair around her gorgeous face. "Thanks," I whispered, unsure of what to say next.

Erin looked so beautiful. I leaned toward her and wrapped my arms around her waist. She inched closer to me, then slowly tilted up her chin.

And then I did it. I kissed her, right there in the street, in front of everyone. And—here's the totally unbelievable part:

She kissed me back.

Bethel

"Bye, Jameel." I smiled into the phone, tracing the receiver with my finger. "I'll see you at school on Monday," I whispered.

"Yeah, see you then," he replied. "I'm glad you called."

"Me too."

I waited a second to see if he'd hang up first. He didn't. *What is my problem?* I scolded myself in annoyance. In thirty-six hours we'd be together again.

"Okay, bye," I said, then quickly hung up before I could stop myself.

Just then the door to our room opened, and Elizabeth and Richard walked in. Elizabeth looked flushed, like she'd just been for a run or something. But Richard looked as cool and calm as ever.

"Hey, Bethel," he greeted me, sitting down in the big armchair by the door.

"Hey," I said, my muscles tightening as I glanced at Elizabeth. I was still kind of annoyed at the way she'd acted today at the capitol.

Elizabeth smiled tentatively. "Hi," she said. "Um, listen, I just wanted to say I'm sorry. You know, about being such a jerk before. It really had nothing to do with you—or even this competition, really."

I shrugged. "It's okay," I told her. "I knew you weren't trying to make me feel bad. I'm kind of sensitive about stuff like that, and I've been stressing about how badly I'm doing."

"Me too." Elizabeth laughed sympathetically. "Richard and I were just talking about that, actually."

"Yeah," Richard added. "We're going to start our own chapter of Academics Anonymous."

I grinned. "Sign me up."

"So are we okay, then?" Elizabeth asked, perching on the edge of her bed.

"Sure," I told her. "And let's make a deal—no matter how we do tomorrow, we won't take it out on each other."

"Agreed," Elizabeth said. "I mean, I'm definitely going to try to do better. But no more crazy obsessive stuff."

"Hey, where's Berna?" Richard asked. "I thought she was crashing early tonight."

I shrugged. "She said she was too wired to sleep, so she went to the lounge to study. She said she'd be back soon." I glanced at my watch. "Wow, it's later than I thought," I said. "No wonder Jameel's mom was yelling at him to get off the phone."

"You talked to Jameel?" Elizabeth's eyes sparkled with interest. "You mean, the guy who isn't your boyfriend?"

"Now you're starting to sound like your twin," I said, frowning. Jessica is always teasing me about Jameel. "Anyway," I continued, heaving my Spanish textbook onto the bed, "we have a big day tomorrow. So I guess I should get back to studying."

"I have a better idea." Richard leaned forward. "Why don't we go out for ice cream—just the three of us? Elizabeth and I were talking about it before."

"Are you nuts?" I checked my watch again. "It's ten-fifteen. The chaperons would freak."

"Richard, you said we could order room service while we studied!" Elizabeth accused.

Richard grinned at her in this crooked way he has. He is pretty adorable, for a locker partner.

Elizabeth sighed. "I guess other people have been sneaking around this whole weekend. And I bet Ms. Upton would let us go anyway if we asked nicely. The worst thing that can happen is she'll say no. What do you think, Bethel?"

"I think you guys are crazy." I laughed, although

they *were* making a pretty good case for ice cream.

"I think it's an important step for the founding members of Academics Anonymous," Richard piped up, his eyes sparkling with laughter. "We need to bond."

I giggled. "Okay, I'm in," I agreed. I followed them out of the room without even a backward glance at my Spanish book.

Elizabeth

"That was the best mint chocolate chip I've ever had," Bethel said as we crossed the hotel lobby to the elevators.

Ms. Upton hadn't been in her room when we'd tried to ask for permission to go out for dessert, but lots of kids that we recognized from the competition seemed to be out around the neighborhood tonight, so we'd figured it was okay. The three of us had all ordered big, yummy sundaes with lots of toppings.

"See? Wasn't that exactly what you needed?" Richard asked, winking at me behind Bethel's back.

Bethel shrugged. "I think going over my Spanish vocab list might have helped me a little more," she answered seriously. Then she laughed. "But sprinkles and whipped cream are definitely more important," she added.

The elevator door opened, and we waited while people poured out, then we stepped inside. Bethel pushed the button for our floor, and Richard hit his.

"Always a pleasure," Richard joked when we got to his floor. He pretended to tip an imaginary hat. I giggled like a silly idiot. Was it my imagination, or did his gaze linger on my face before he waved good-bye?

I shook my head as the door slid shut behind him. My imagination was in high gear tonight.

The elevator reached our floor, and Bethel and I started walking to our room. As we rounded the corner, I caught sight of Ms. Upton talking to someone. Her back was to us, but Bethel and I froze. Bethel glanced at me questioningly, and I quickly darted behind a big potted plant. Bethel was close behind me.

"You should not be on the girls' floor at this hour," I heard Ms. Upton reprimand someone. Bethel and I exchanged a curious glance. At least Richard hadn't come back with us, or he would have been in trouble.

Ms. Upton finished her lecture, and we heard her door slam shut. Then we peeked around the plant to make sure the hallway was clear.

I gasped when I saw who was walking down the hallway toward us, his eyes trained on the floor.

"Salvador?" I blurted out.

His head jerked up, and he caught my eye. "Elizabeth?"

Bethel and I stepped out from behind the plant.

"Hey, Salvador," Bethel said, brushing off a leaf from her shirt. She smiled at him. "Ms. Upton giving you a hard time?"

Salvador stared at us. "Why were you guys *hiding?*" he asked.

I shrugged. "We just got back from getting ice cream," I explained. "We weren't sure if Ms. Upton would be mad."

"Well, looks like I saved you guys," he said. "She was too busy yelling at me for . . ." He trailed off and looked away.

He was with Erin, I realized. He'd probably walked her back to her room after spending the whole night hanging out with her. And he was afraid I'd be upset.

Well, aren't I?

I bit my lip as I thought about it. Watching Salvador with Erin had been driving me crazy all weekend. But I'd had my own good time with Richard and then later with Bethel too.

"Did you . . . have a good night?" I asked Salvador in my best I'm-so-friendly voice. I noticed Bethel's eyes widen slightly. She probably figured I was ready to blow up at him or something. I guess Salvador did too because he squinted at me without answering for a few seconds, like he was trying to see if I meant it.

"Yeah, I did, actually," he replied. "Did you?"

I smiled. "Yeah, we did," I said.

Salvador nodded. "Cool."

We stood there for a moment, and then Bethel let out a sigh. "Well, I think we've been outrageous enough for one night," she said. "Let's get back to our rooms, okay?"

"Good idea," I agreed. I smiled at Salvador. I felt like we were okay now. I hoped he did too. "Good night," I told him.

"See you tomorrow," he said, smiling back. Then he turned and walked over to the elevators.

"That was weird," Bethel whispered to me outside our door. "You really don't mind that he was obviously with Erin?"

I shook my head. "You know, I really don't," I said, pulling my key out of my pocket.

It is weird, though, I realized. I'd thought this trip was going to be a chance for me and Salvador to see if we could be more than "just friends."

But instead I'd found that "friends" is exactly what we were meant to be. (And there were no "justs" about it.)

Sacramento at Midnight

Hi, Jameel,

I'm never sure what to write on postcards. The whole postcard concept is actually pretty weird if you think about it, you know? I mean, everybody at the post office can just read whatever you write if they feel like it.

So I guess I'll just talk to you when I get home.

Bethel

P.S. Sorry the picture on this card is so lame.

Salvador

"And finally," Dr. Trask began. "Let me announce the winner of the science competition." It was Sunday afternoon, and the testing had wrapped up a couple of hours ago. Now the whole group was assembled back in the banquet room to find out the winners in every subject, and science was last. We sat by topic, so I hadn't been able to see the expressions on my teammates' faces when their names *weren't* called, but I figured none of them was too surprised. I did, however, see Ronald's eager race to the stage when he snagged first place in math.

I leaned back in my seat as Dr. Trask opened an envelope and pulled out a slip of paper. I certainly wasn't expecting to hear my name since I'd messed up even more questions today than I had yesterday.

"Erin Dunkerly from Smithfield Junior High," he said.

I sat up and let out a whistle. "Way to go, Erin!" I shouted. But so many other people were clapping and cheering that she probably couldn't hear me. At least, I figured that's why she didn't turn toward me. Weird, though—we were only a few seats apart.

Erin stepped up onto the stage and accepted the award from the judge. By the time she climbed back down, everyone was up from their seats and the room was complete chaos.

I wandered through the crowd, trying to get near Erin to congratulate her. I don't know how she'd managed to do so well without getting enough sleep or doing any studying, but obviously the girl was a genius. A beautiful genius. Who kissed me . . .

"Hey, Erin," I called out as I caught a glimpse of her long, dark hair gleaming in the lights. "Let's meet out . . ."

My voice trailed off as she swept right past me without a glance. A second later she disappeared through the door.

I just stood there, confused. She'd passed within three feet of me—she had to have seen me. And she definitely heard me. So why had she ignored me like that?

Suddenly a sickening idea struck me. What if Erin had spent all that time with me just to get rid of the competition so she'd have a better chance of winning?

Sinking into a chair, I let my head drop into my hands, feeling like I'd just been run over by a big, stinky garbage truck. Maybe I was just being paranoid, but why else would she forget I existed as soon as she had her trophy?

I thought Erin was for real, but even *I'd* had trouble believing a girl like her actually liked me. *That's probably because she didn't,* I thought with disgust.

Then I thought about my teammates from SVJH—I'd let them down, and for someone who didn't even care about me at all.

I let Elizabeth down, I thought as I pictured the way she'd smiled at me last night in the hallway, obviously trying to let me know she wasn't mad anymore.

I hopped out of my seat. *Boy, have I been a moron,* I thought as I scanned the large room for Elizabeth. *Here I wasted all this time on Erin, who was only using me. And I could have been hanging out with Elizabeth all along!*

There was only one thing to do—I had to find Elizabeth. The weekend wasn't over yet.

Damon

"Can you get that, Damon?" my mother called from her bedroom as the doorbell buzzed on Sunday afternoon. "It's probably Ben. Tell him I'll be right out."

I got up from the couch and strolled over to the door. I swung it open and frowned when I saw Ben's smiling, hairy face.

"Come in," I said bluntly, not bothering to return the smile. "Mom's almost ready."

Sally and Kaia looked up from some kiddie show they were watching and squealed with delight. "Ben!" they shouted in unison, and ran over to fling themselves at his legs. I headed down the hall and knocked on my mom's half-open door. She was standing in front of her mirror, wearing her favorite red dress, dabbing perfume on her wrists.

She glanced up at me. "Come on in," she said cheerfully. "Is Ben here?"

"Uh-huh." I took a deep breath, still hovering in the doorway. "Um, listen, Mom," I blurted out.

152

"Is Ben going to become an everyday thing now?"

She blinked and turned away from the mirror to face me. "What are you talking about, sweetie?" she asked with a laugh. "Ben and I are going out tonight to make up for missing our date last night. That's all."

"Really?" I glanced over my shoulder toward the main room to make sure Ben wasn't listening. He was busy with the girls. "That's twice in one weekend. Seems kind of serious."

She laughed again, her eyes twinkling. "Serious?" she exclaimed. "Are you kidding? We've only been out twice!"

I blushed, feeling stupid for being so neurotic.

"Damon, Ben and I are friends. We're still getting to know each other. I'm not about to run off and get married again." She smiled at me. "You're still the main man in my life."

Relief washed over me. Maybe I really *had* been making a huge deal out of nothing. Mom sounded like she knew what she was doing. And she understood why I was worried about her too.

"Okay. Sorry," I said. "Have fun."

"Thanks, Dad," she replied, laughing.

Still getting to know each other, I thought, heading into my room. I could handle that. That could take a long time. It sure had with me and Jessica.

Damon

I sank down on my bed, wincing as I thought about the way my date with Jessica ended last night.

I glanced at my phone. Then I took a deep breath and grabbed it, dialing her number.

"Hello?" Jessica answered after a couple of rings.

"Hi, it's Damon," I said. Silence. "I just wanted to say that I'm really, really sorry about last night. And the night before too."

"Oh?" she asked flatly. There was a coldness in her voice that I'd never heard before. This was going to be tough.

I swallowed. "See," I said, "I was kind of freaked out about my mom dating this guy, Ben."

Jessica paused. "You were acting like that be-cause of your *mom?*" she asked suspiciously.

"Yeah," I said.

"What about last night? You said she was at work."

"She was. But Ben was baby-sitting. I think he and my mom are kind of . . . starting something." I stopped, wondering how much I could tell her. "See, um, when my dad left . . . well, my mom was really messed up, and so were my sisters. I just don't want that to happen to any of them again. It's hard when you think someone's going to be around, and then suddenly they're gone." My voice got kind of hoarse, and I cleared my throat.

154

"Damon . . . I'm sorry," Jessica said. "I thought you just didn't want to be around me."

"No way," I said. *It's all I want!* I added inwardly. "So, you're not mad?" I asked.

"No," she replied. "Thanks for telling me what was going on." Her voice sounded soft, and I wished she was right there so I could give her a hug.

"Sure," I said. "Listen, I should probably say something nice to Ben before he and my mom leave. But I'll call you later, okay?"

"Uh-huh. Bye, Damon. And let me know how things go, okay?"

"Yeah." I smiled. "Thanks, Jess. Bye." I hung up, then sat there, staring at the phone for a second.

I felt way, way better than I'd felt like fifteen minutes ago. Thanks to Mom. And even more thanks to Jessica. I was going to make it up to her too. I just had to think of the best way to do it.

Bethel

"I still can't believe I choked," I muttered, flinging a T-shirt into my suitcase.

Elizabeth shot me a sympathetic glance. She was stuffing her dirty clothes into a plastic bag. "I know how you feel," she said.

"That makes three of us," Bernadette put in quietly from her spot on the bed. She'd already finished packing.

None of us had even placed high enough to get honorable-mention ribbons. I was holding to the deal not to flip out on Elizabeth or anyone else, but instead I was flipping out on *myself*, big time.

"Well, anyway," Elizabeth said, "at least Ronald isn't holding any grudges against us for blowing his chances of a team medal on top of his individual one." I snorted, and we all laughed.

Ronald had won the math competition, of course. The next-best scorer from our group was Richard, who'd ended up in fifteenth place. Elizabeth and Bernadette both placed eighteenth. I scored twenty-fifth. And Salvador . . . Well, let's just say he made the rest of us look like geniuses.

"This stinks," I said, kicking my extra shoes out from under the corner of the bed. "I mean, our whole team should have just stayed home."

Elizabeth glanced at me. "I don't know about that."

I shrugged. "Yeah, you're right," I grumbled. "We should have just sent Ronald."

"No," Elizabeth said. "That's not what I meant. I meant that I'm still glad we came. We had fun, right?"

Bernadette nodded, but I just stared at Elizabeth blankly. "Fun?" I repeated.

"Yeah." Elizabeth grinned. "We saw a whole new city and met people from all over the state. We got to stay in this cool hotel without any of our parents around. Come on, Bethel, remember that mint-chocolate-chip ice cream last night?"

I smiled despite myself. "It was good," I admitted. "But we didn't come here for *fun*. Or for ice cream," I added.

"So what?" Elizabeth asked. "At least we got something out of it."

I thought about that for a second. Was having fun really enough to make up for losing?

I started to smile. Then I broke into a laugh.

"What's so funny?" Bernadette asked.

"*We* are," I replied between giggles. "What a pathetic bunch of overachievers!"

I kept laughing, and Elizabeth and Bernadette joined in. Here we were, some of the best students in our entire school. And we'd come out looking like a bunch of goof-offs who wouldn't know an A if we tripped over one.

As I remembered some of the stupid, silly mistakes I'd made over the past two days and the way I'd practically forgotten my own name every time I saw that guy who looked like Jameel, I couldn't help laughing even harder. Soon we were all practically rolling on the floor.

Finally I got control of myself again. "Whew!" I gasped as I zipped my bag shut. "You know, I was so nervous this morning, I hardly ate breakfast. Want to go grab something in the coffee shop? We still have some time before we have to meet the bus."

"Sure," Bernadette said.

But Elizabeth shook her head, glancing down at her suitcase. "I'd better finish packing first," she said. "And then I'm supposed to meet Richard for lunch."

"Okay." I smiled at her, glad that I'd gotten the chance to know her better. Maybe she and I would never be best friends or anything, but she wasn't just "Jessica's twin sister" anymore. She was a pretty cool person.

And she was right—I *was* glad I'd come on this trip.

Elizabeth

I was in the bathroom, retrieving my shampoo from the shower, when I heard a knock on the room door. Bethel and Bernadette had already gone downstairs.

"Hold on," I called.

"Elizabeth?" The voice was muffled, but I could tell it was Salvador. I hurried over to open the door.

"Hi," I said when I saw him. "What's up?"

He shuffled from one foot to the other. "Can I come in?" he asked.

"Sure." I stood back to let him in. "Is something wrong?"

He walked over to one of the dressers and leaned against it. "You know that girl Erin I've been hanging around with?" He shot me a sidelong glance.

I could tell that he was sort of expecting me to freak out—get mad, or act jealous, or something like that. But I could honestly say that I was just worried about him. He looked really upset.

"Yeah, she seemed nice. What happened?" I asked.

He blinked in surprise. "Uh, she blew me off after the competition today." He shook his head. "Just ran by me like I wasn't even there. I think maybe she was only hanging around me to keep me from studying so that she'd have an easy shot at first place."

"What?" That didn't sound right. "Are you sure about that? Because she—she really looked like she was into you." I remembered the way Salvador and Erin had been all snuggled up on the couch in the lobby yesterday. There was a reason it got to me so much—I could tell that they really, really liked each other.

Salvador shrugged. "She definitely didn't want to talk to me today. What other reason is there?"

"There could be other reasons." I tried to think. "Maybe she was so overwhelmed about winning that she didn't see you," I suggested. "Or maybe she was rushing to call her parents and give them the news. Think about it—why would she pick you to distract out of everyone else in the competition? It doesn't really make sense. Besides, you weren't exactly in *second* place there, Sal."

Salvador didn't look convinced. "Well, anyway," he said, "I'm sorry I've been acting so lame." He bit his lip and stared at me. "I mean, I wish we hadn't had that stupid fight. Then you and I could have spent the whole weekend together like I thought we would."

I looked away, shocked to hear what I'd been thinking before we got on the bus on Friday. How could I tell him I was glad things turned out the way they did? Not that I'd liked being mad at Salvador or anything. But if we hadn't had that fight, I might not have spent so much time getting to know Richard and Bethel. And I wouldn't have realized that I wanted to remain "just friends"—at least for now—with Salvador.

But I couldn't come out and say that, not when Salvador was already so upset.

"Don't worry," I said. "I'm not mad anymore."

"Really?" he asked, sounding surprised.

"We're definitely okay." Glancing at the clock on the bedside table, I suddenly remembered I had to meet Richard. "Oops," I said. "Listen, I really have to go. I told Richard I'd meet him for lunch. We can talk about this more on the bus if you want."

Salvador's eyes widened in surprise, but he nodded. "Sure," he said. "I'll save you a spot on the bus. Have fun at lunch, okay?"

"Don't worry, I will." I smiled as he headed out the door.

I bent down to zip my bag shut and noticed a

pink-and-black-striped sock under the bed—
Bernadette's. Grabbing it, I surveyed the rest of
the room to see if we'd missed anything else.
Then I glanced back at the sock. There was a little pink bow at the heel. A smile crept across my
face, and then I just started laughing—really,
really hard.

Sacramento at Midnight

Dear Anna,
  Well, this turned out to be a really great trip in the end. I wish you could have been here—maybe next time they'll add a category for poetry. You might even win your event and redeem SVGH's reputation—unfortunately most of us (except Ronald) didn't do too well. Oh well, better luck next year. . .

  There's not much room on this card, but I probably will have told you everything by the time you get this anyway. See you soon!

                    Your friend always,
                    Elizabeth

Salvador

What just happened? I wondered as I ambled my way down the hall away from Elizabeth's room. *I thought I was going in to beg Elizabeth to give me another chance. But instead I wound up telling her about Erin. . . .*

I scuffed my toe on the rug. After Erin blew me off, I'd immediately thought how I should have been with Elizabeth all along. But talking to Elizabeth just now hadn't felt like it used to. That weird, fluttery, breathless feeling, like my heart just sped up a few notches—it wasn't there. Even when I looked into her pretty blue-green eyes, all I could think about was *Erin*.

I was totally relieved that Elizabeth wasn't mad at me because she's one of my best friends. But—for the first time ever—that was all I wanted her to be.

The sound of laughter jolted me out of my thoughts. Glancing down the hall, I saw a cluster of girls lugging their suitcases out of a room at the far end.

As soon as I recognized Erin, my heart skipped a beat. Then that feeling—the one I hadn't felt with Elizabeth—came over me. It was like I could barely breathe.

Erin turned her head and spotted me. She stopped short, nearly dropping her suitcase on the floor. Then she turned to her friends and said something I couldn't hear. After a quick glance at me they hurried away in the other direction, and she hurried toward me.

I couldn't take my eyes off her. She looked beautiful, as always. But as she got closer, I saw that her eyes weren't all bright and sparkly like they usually were.

"Hi," she said. "Uh, how's it going?"

I shrugged. I wanted to say something cool and casual and maybe a little mean, like, *It's going, and so am I.* But I couldn't get the words out.

"Fine," I mumbled.

"Listen, Sal," she said hesitantly. "About this morning, when I didn't talk to you after the competition—I know that was pretty rude. It's just . . ."

"What?" I prompted after a moment of silence. I couldn't help hoping that Elizabeth was right—that Erin hadn't been using me. But I was prepared for the worst.

She cleared her throat. "Well, I guess I sort of

165

freaked out," she said. "It suddenly seemed so weird—I mean, we might never see each other again!"

"Really?" I asked in amazement. "That's why you didn't talk to me?"

She nodded and smiled faintly. "Pretty lame, huh? I mean, it's not like we both didn't know this couldn't last."

"Yeah." It was true. I hadn't let myself think about it, but we lived at opposite ends of the state. I couldn't exactly take Erin to the next school dance or anything. I was just so relieved to hear that she hadn't ignored me because she didn't like me—but because she *really* liked me a lot.

"Still, I'm glad I met you," I said. "This weekend was the best."

She took a step closer. "Definitely," she agreed, giggling. "So maybe we can do it again next year?"

"Don't count on it," I joked. "After how I did this year, I'm surprised I didn't get arrested for disorderly conduct." Ms. Upton had already informed me that we'd be having a "conversation" in school Monday about the way I had "failed to appreciate the gravity" of the competition.

Erin laughed. Then her face composed itself into a beautiful display of sadness, happiness, and regret—everything I felt inside. "Bye, Salvador," she said. "I'll miss you."

"Me too." I put my hands on her waist, right there in the middle of the hall. She put her arms around my shoulders and looked up at me, her eyes locked on mine. Pulling her closer, I leaned down and kissed her. Her lips were soft and warm, and I closed my eyes and just sank into the feeling.

We pulled apart way too soon.

"Good-bye," I said again, my voice cracking.

Erin smiled. "Bye."

Then she turned around and walked back down the hall to get her suitcase, and I walked the other way toward the elevators. I still had to finish packing all my stuff, but somehow I couldn't face the hotel room right then.

Snack bar, I thought, hitting the down button on the wall next to the elevator. Maybe if I ate something, it would help with this hollow feeling in my stomach.

I got off the elevator in the lobby and glanced out through the glass doors, spotting a bunch of buses lined up in front of the hotel. Smiling, I headed toward the snack machines where I'd met Erin.

It had been an interesting weekend—kind of like a new beginning. I couldn't wait to get back to SVJH and try out the new me.

Check out the **all-new** ....

(**Sweet Valley Web site—**)

www.sweetvalley.com

New Features

Cool Prizes

The **ONLY** official Web site!

Hot Links

(And much more!)

You hate your **alarm clock.**

You hate your **clothes.**

You're going
to love
Jr. High.